WITHDRAWN

BABYMOUSE AND FRIENDS*

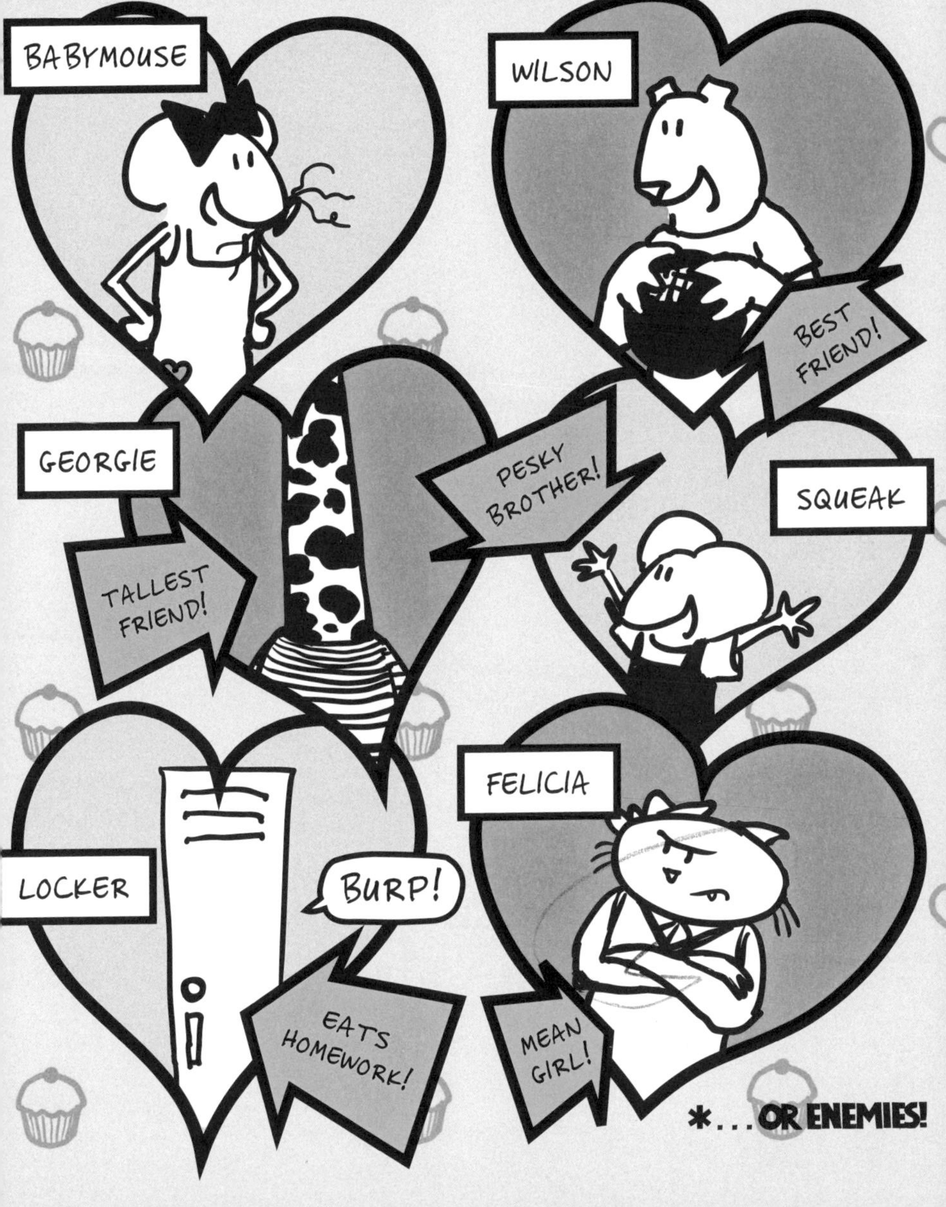
BABYMOUSE
WILSON
BEST FRIEND!
GEORGIE
TALLEST FRIEND!
PESKY BROTHER!
SQUEAK
LOCKER
BURP!
EATS HOMEWORK!
FELICIA
MEAN GIRL!

*. . . OR ENEMIES!

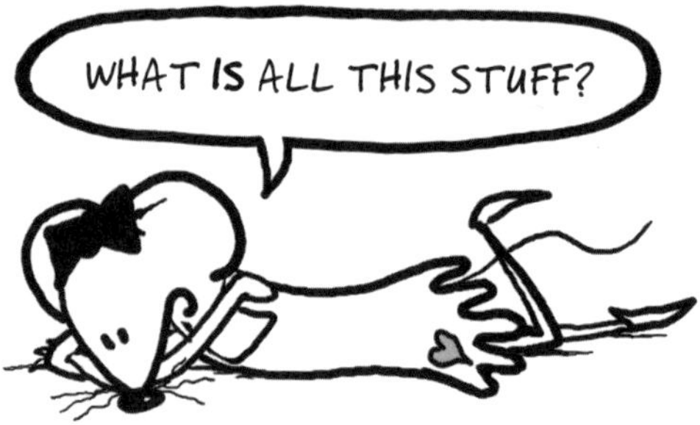
WHAT IS ALL THIS STUFF?

Be sure to read **ALL** the **BABYMOUSE** books:

#1 BABYMOUSE: Queen of the World!
#2 BABYMOUSE: Our Hero
#3 BABYMOUSE: Beach Babe
#4 BABYMOUSE: Rock Star
#5 BABYMOUSE: Heartbreaker
#6 CAMP BABYMOUSE
#7 BABYMOUSE: Skater Girl
#8 BABYMOUSE: Puppy Love
#9 BABYMOUSE: Monster Mash
#10 BABYMOUSE: The Musical
#11 BABYMOUSE: Dragonslayer
#12 BABYMOUSE: Burns Rubber
#13 BABYMOUSE: Cupcake Tycoon
#14 BABYMOUSE: Mad Scientist
#15 A Very BABYMOUSE Christmas
#16 BABYMOUSE for President
#17 Extreme BABYMOUSE
#18 Happy Birthday, BABYMOUSE

BABYMOUSE
ROCK STAR

BY JENNIFER L. HOLM & MATTHEW HOLM

RANDOM HOUSE NEW YORK

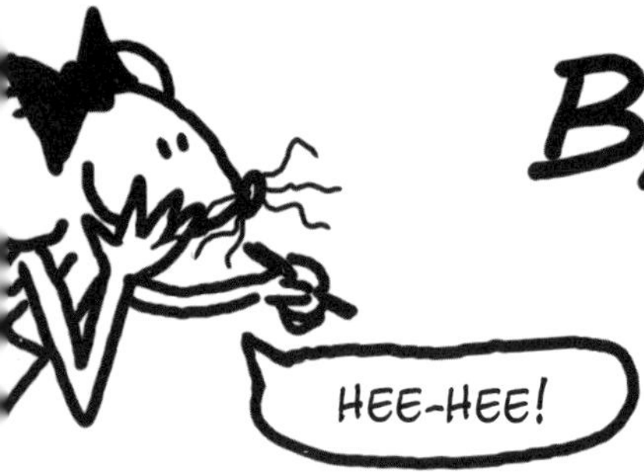
HEE-HEE!

BABYMOUSE WUZ HERE

This is a work of fiction. Names, characters, places, and incidents either are the product of the authors' imagination or are used fictitiously. Any resemblance to actual persons, living or dead, events, or locales is entirely coincidental.

Published in the United States by Random House Children's Books, a division of Penguin Random House LLC, New York.

Random House and the colophon are registered trademarks of Penguin Random House LLC.

Visit us on the Web!
randomhousekids.com
Babymouse.com

Educators and librarians, for a variety of teaching tools, visit us at RHTeachersLibrarians.com

Library of Congress Cataloging-in-Publication Data
Holm, Jennifer L.
Babymouse : rock star / Jennifer Holm and Matthew Holm.
p. cm.
ISBN 978-0-375-83232-1 (trade) — ISBN 978-0-375-93232-8 (lib. bdg.)
ISBN 978-0-307-97929-2 (ebook)
1. Graphic novels. I. Holm, Matthew. II. Title.
PN6727.H592B34 2006
741.5'973—dc22
2005046464

MANUFACTURED IN MALAYSIA 25 24 23 22 21 20 19 18 17 16

Random House Children's Books supports the First Amendment and celebrates the right to read.

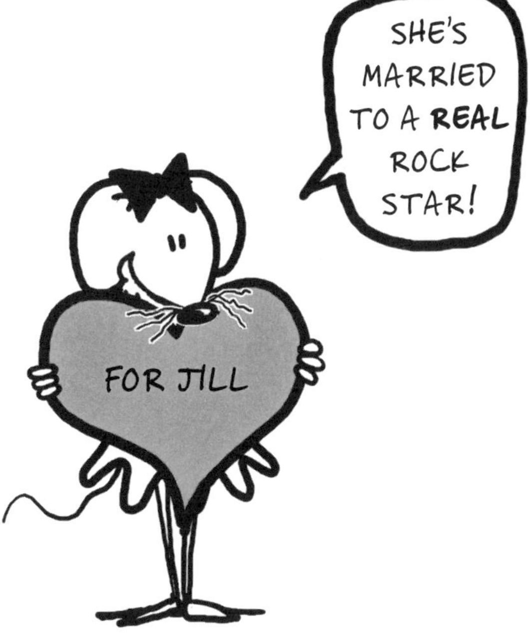
SHE'S MARRIED TO A **REAL** ROCK STAR!
FOR JILL

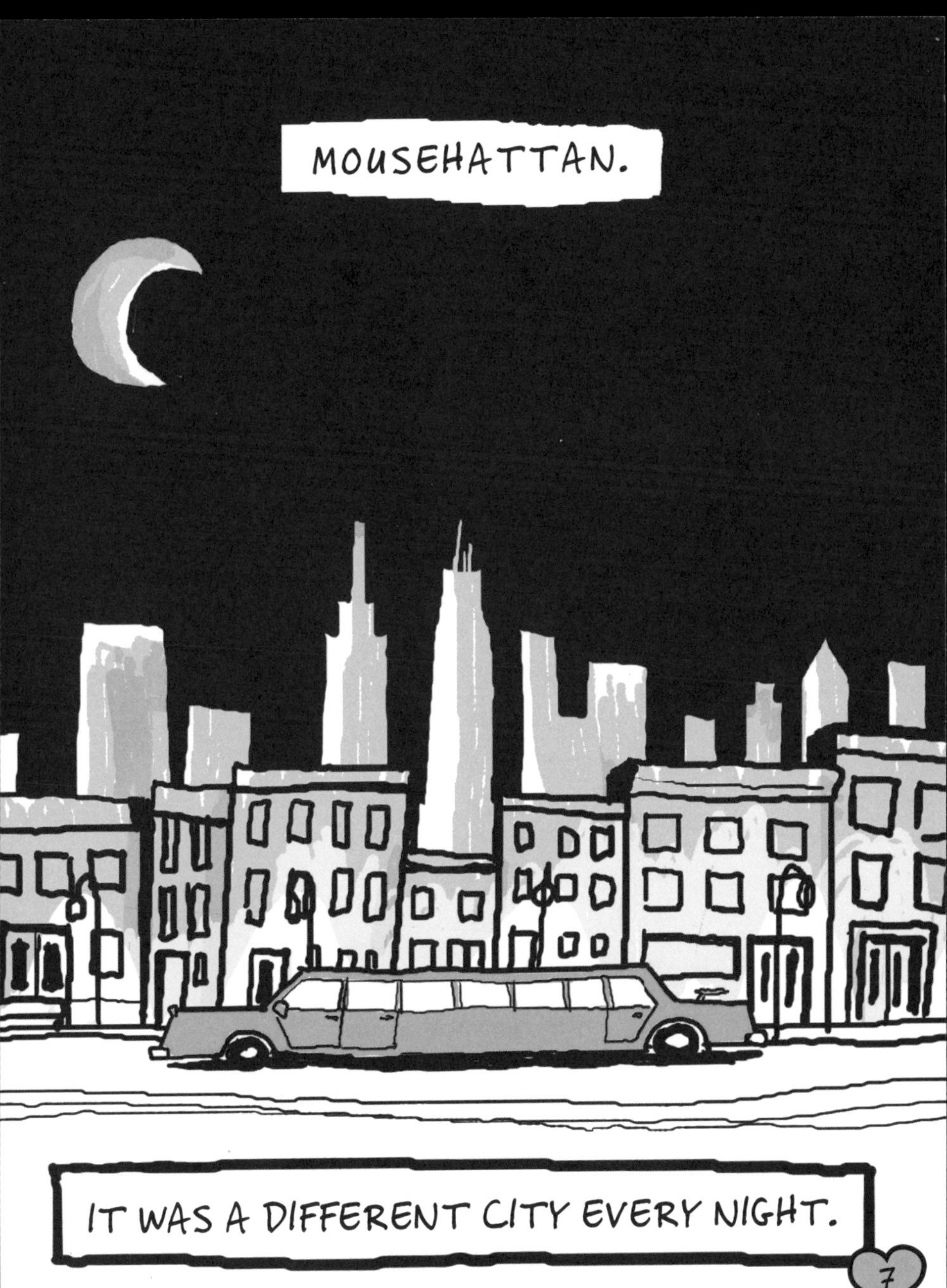
MOUSEHATTAN.
IT WAS A DIFFERENT CITY EVERY NIGHT.

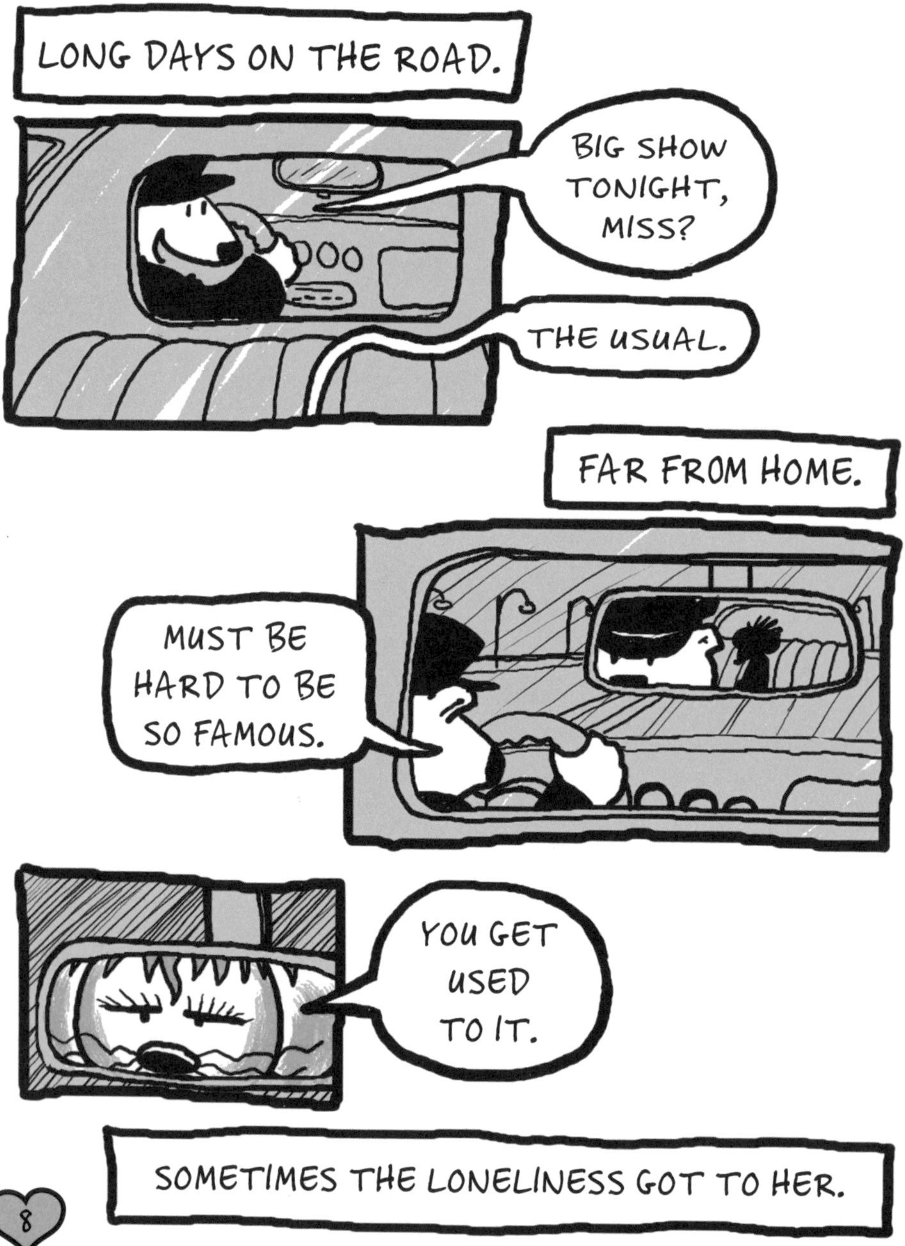
LONG DAYS ON THE ROAD.
BIG SHOW TONIGHT, MISS?
THE USUAL.
FAR FROM HOME.
MUST BE HARD TO BE SO FAMOUS.
YOU GET USED TO IT.
SOMETIMES THE LONELINESS GOT TO HER.

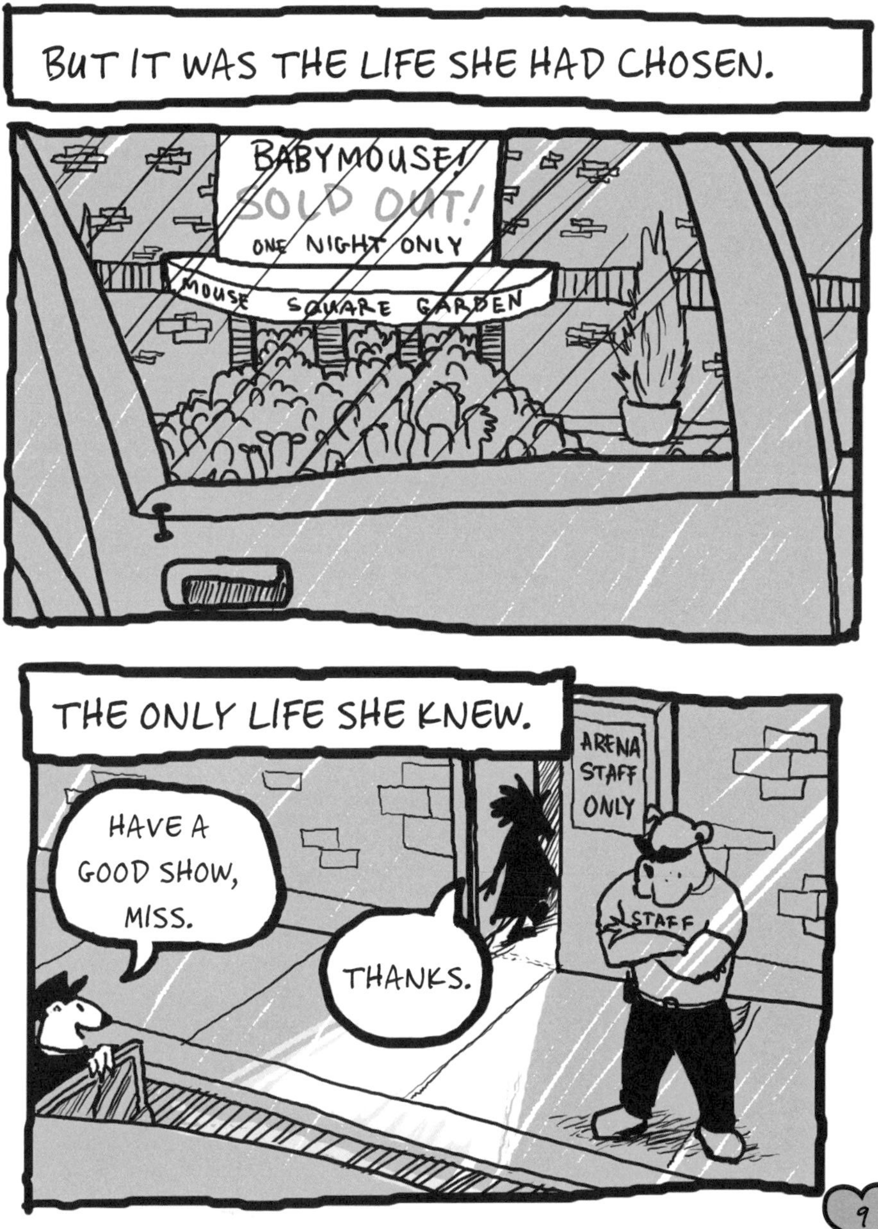
BUT IT WAS THE LIFE SHE HAD CHOSEN.
BABYMOUSE!
SOLD OUT!
ONE NIGHT ONLY
MOUSE SQUARE GARDEN
THE ONLY LIFE SHE KNEW.
ARENA STAFF ONLY
HAVE A GOOD SHOW, MISS.
THANKS.
STAFF

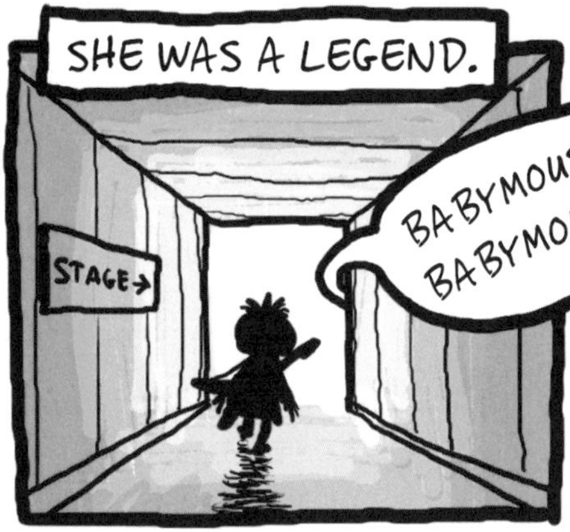
SHE WAS A LEGEND.
STAGE →
BABYMOUSE! BABYMOUSE!

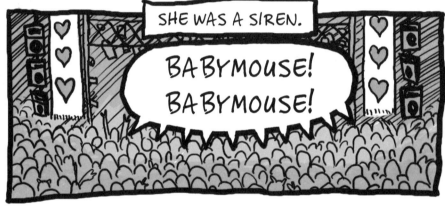

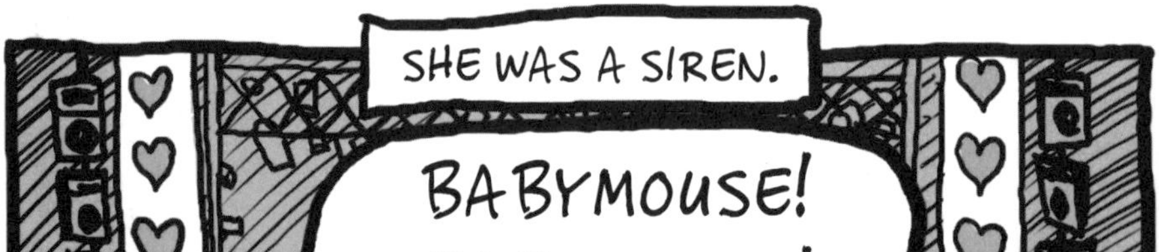
SHE WAS A SIREN.
BABYMOUSE! BABYMOUSE!

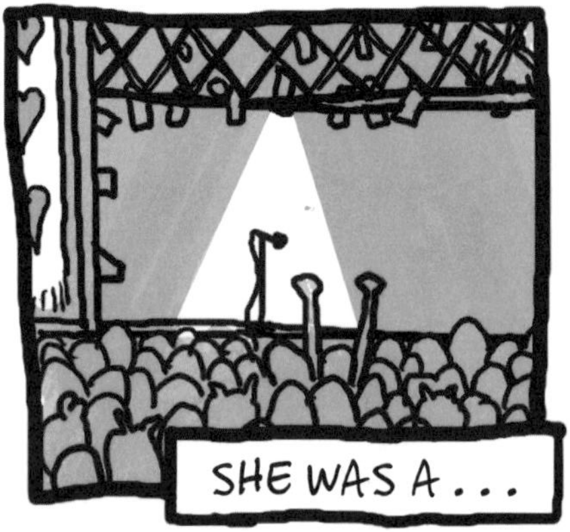
SHE WAS A . . .

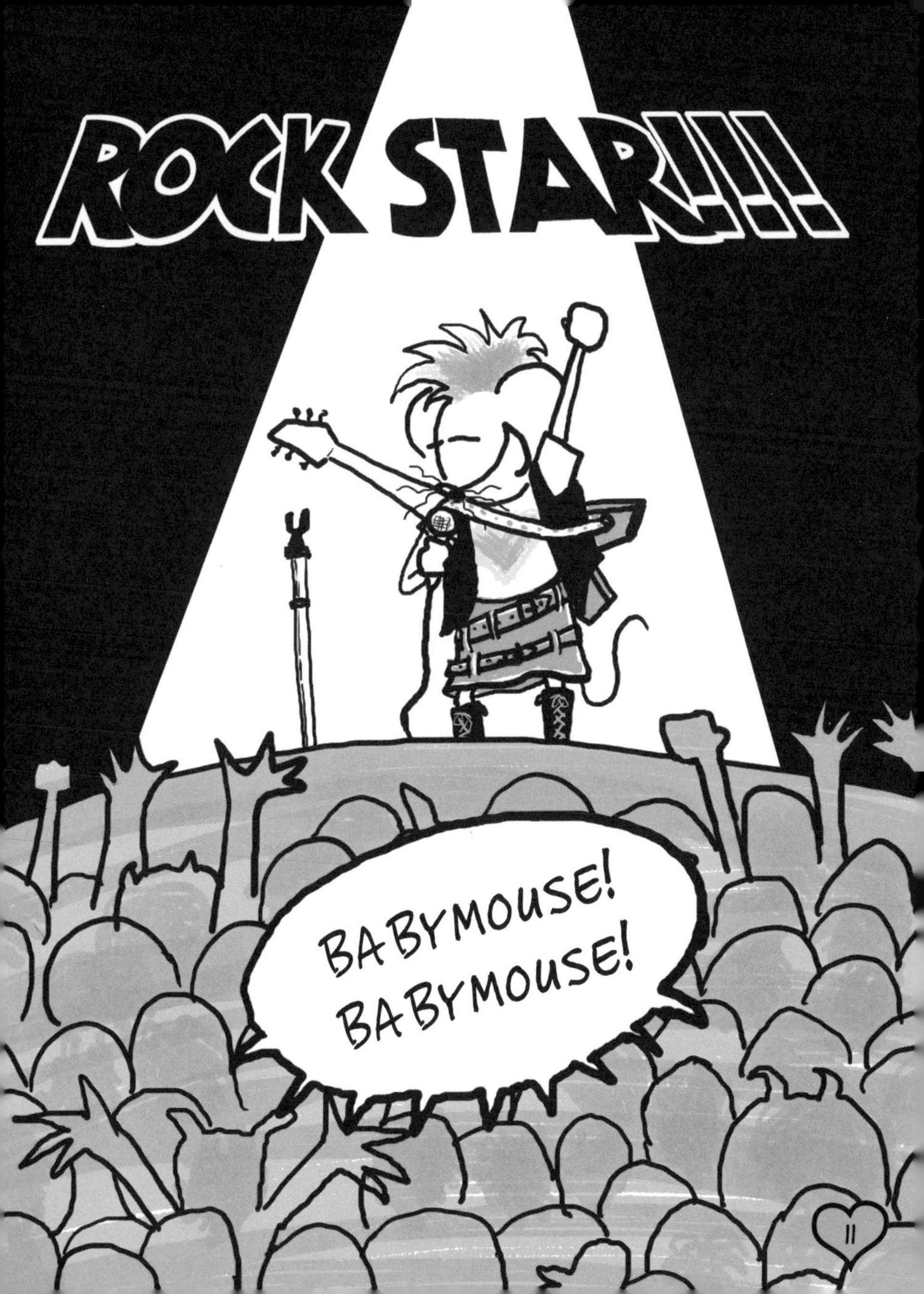
ROCK STAR!!!!
BABYMOUSE! BABYMOUSE!

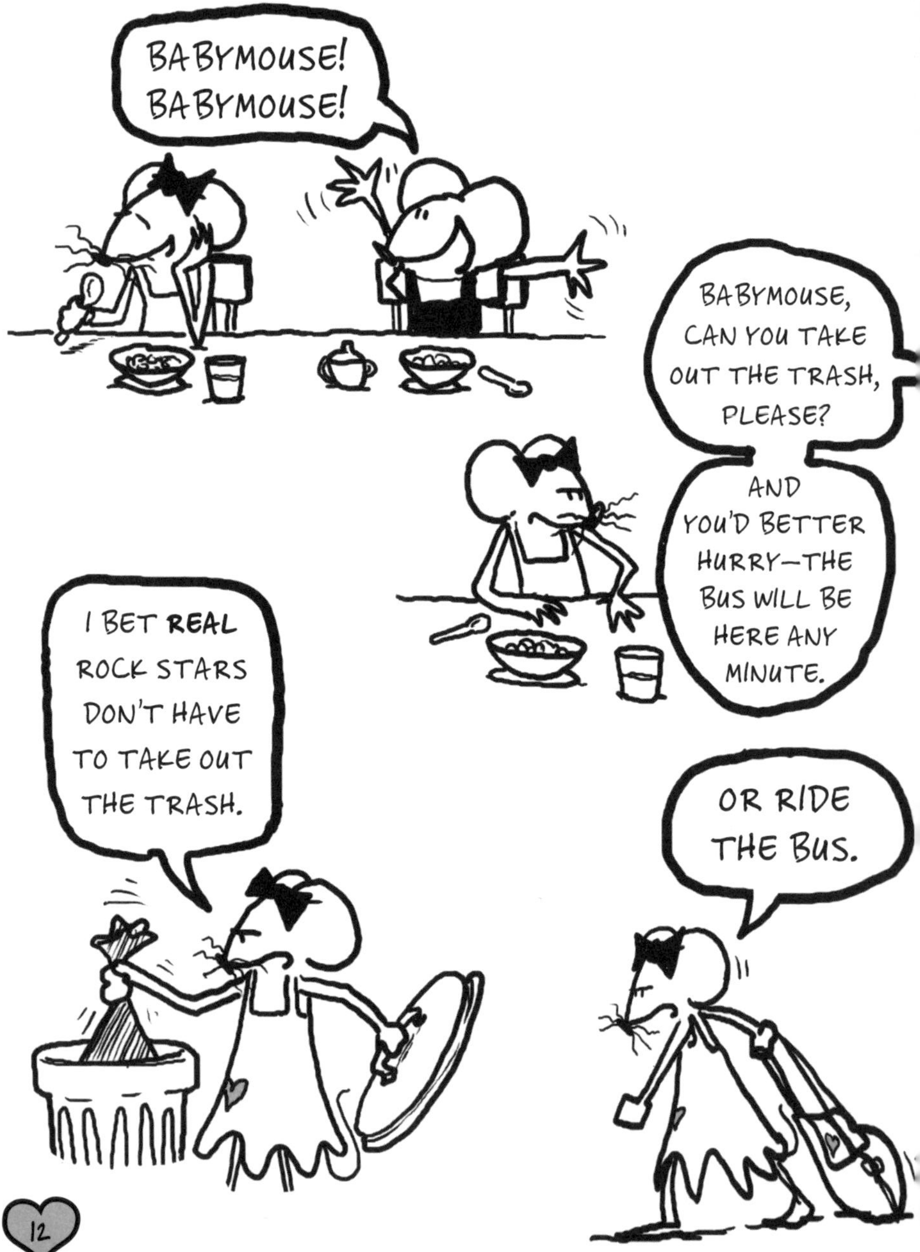
BABYMOUSE! BABYMOUSE!
BABYMOUSE, CAN YOU TAKE OUT THE TRASH, PLEASE?
AND YOU'D BETTER HURRY—THE BUS WILL BE HERE ANY MINUTE.
I BET **REAL** ROCK STARS DON'T HAVE TO TAKE OUT THE TRASH.
OR RIDE THE BUS.

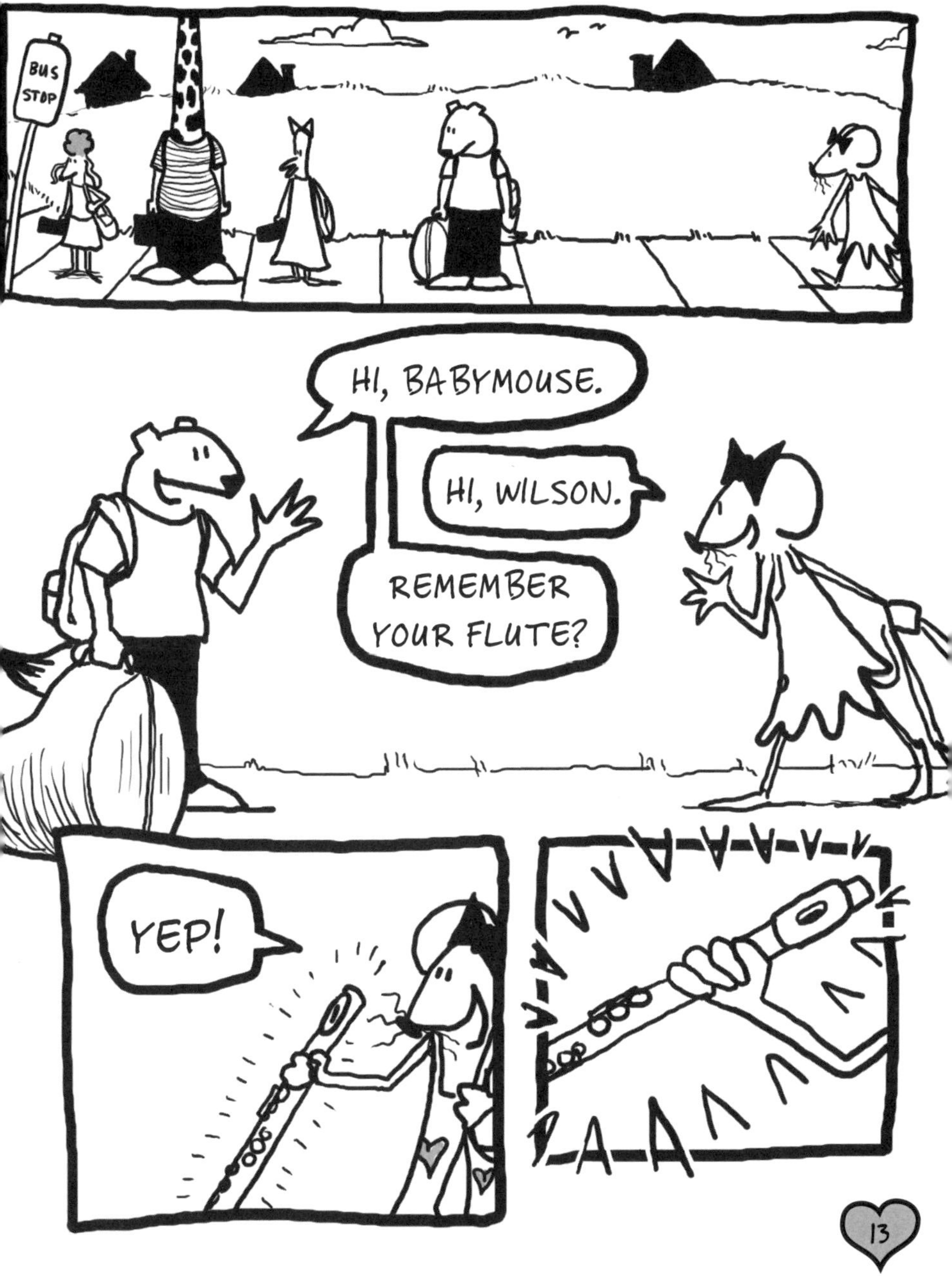
BUS STOP
HI, BABYMOUSE.
HI, WILSON.
REMEMBER YOUR FLUTE?
YEP!

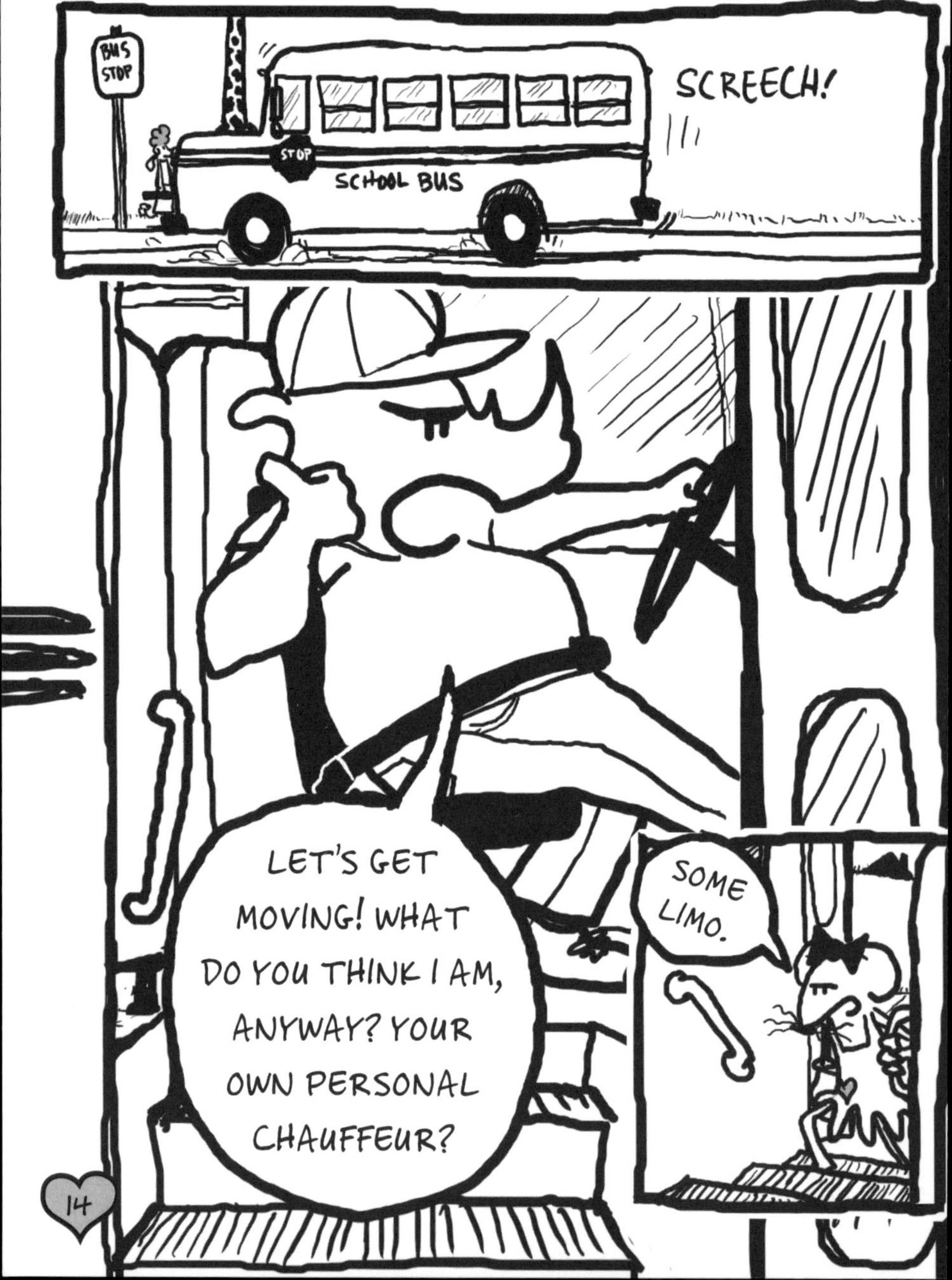
BUS STOP
STOP
SCHOOL BUS
SCREECH!
LET'S GET MOVING! WHAT DO YOU THINK I AM, ANYWAY? YOUR OWN PERSONAL CHAUFFEUR?
SOME LIMO.

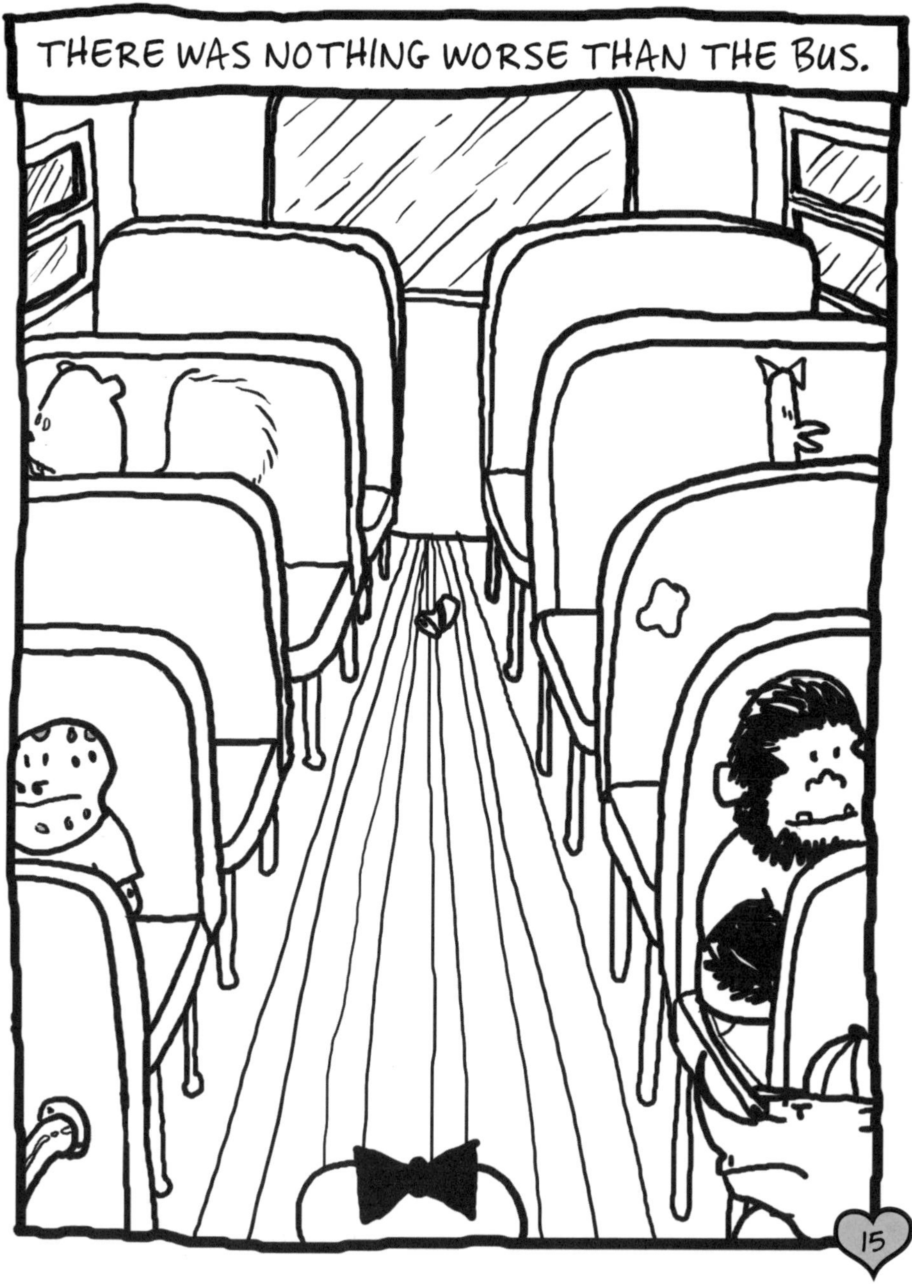
THERE WAS NOTHING WORSE THAN THE BUS.

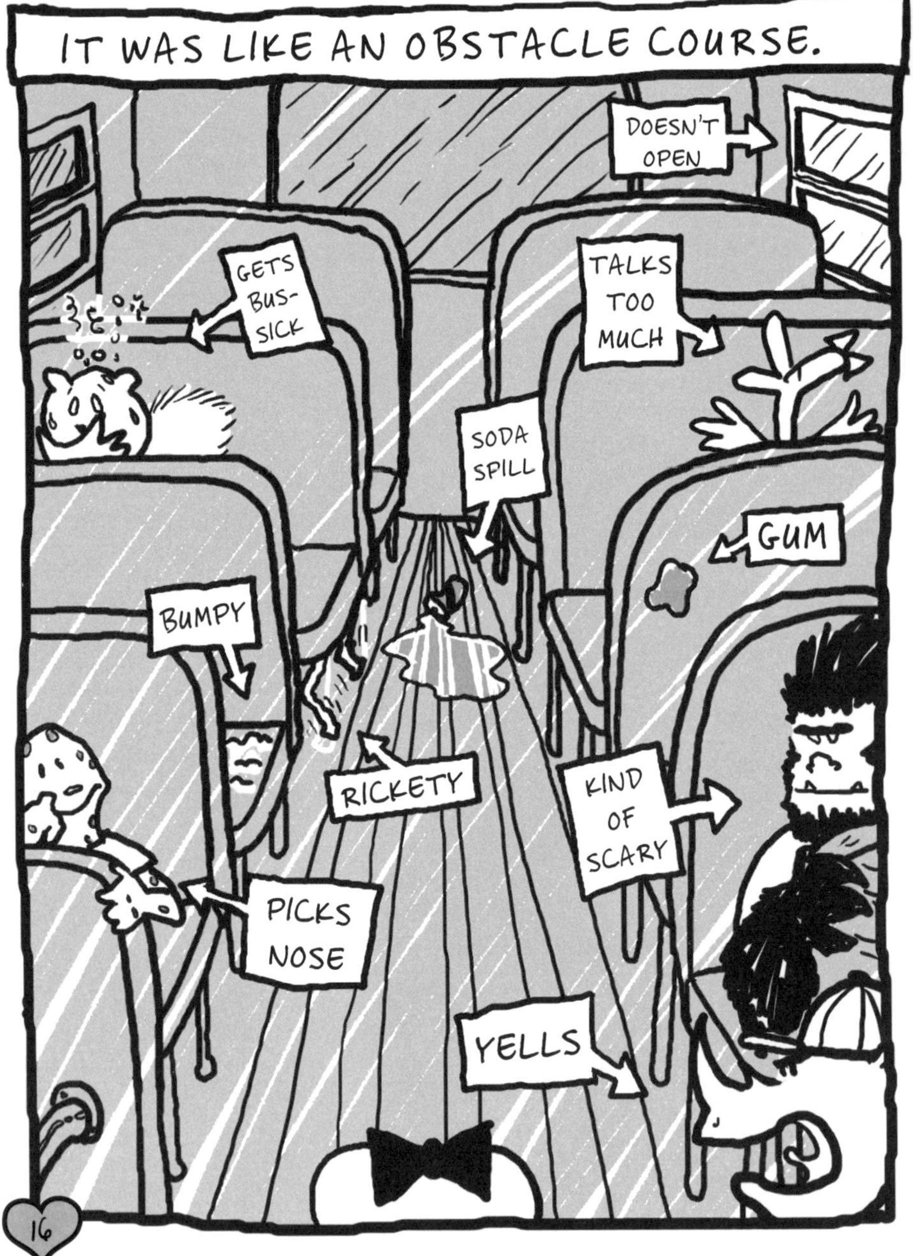
IT WAS LIKE AN OBSTACLE COURSE.
DOESN'T OPEN
GETS BUS-SICK
TALKS TOO MUCH
SODA SPILL
GUM
BUMPY
RICKETY
KIND OF SCARY
PICKS NOSE
YELLS

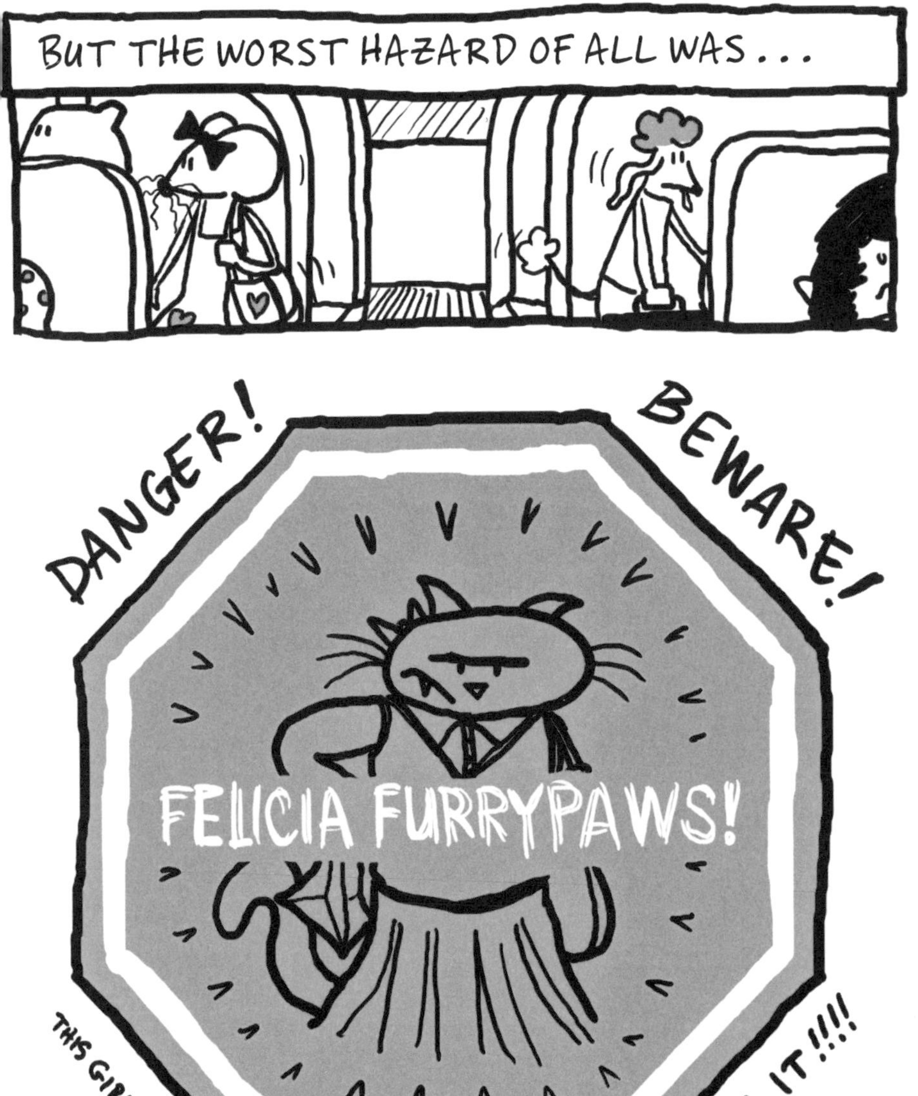

BUT THE WORST HAZARD OF ALL WAS . . .
DANGER!
BEWARE!
FELICIA FURRYPAWS!
THIS GIRL'S TROUBLE!
WE MEAN IT!!!!

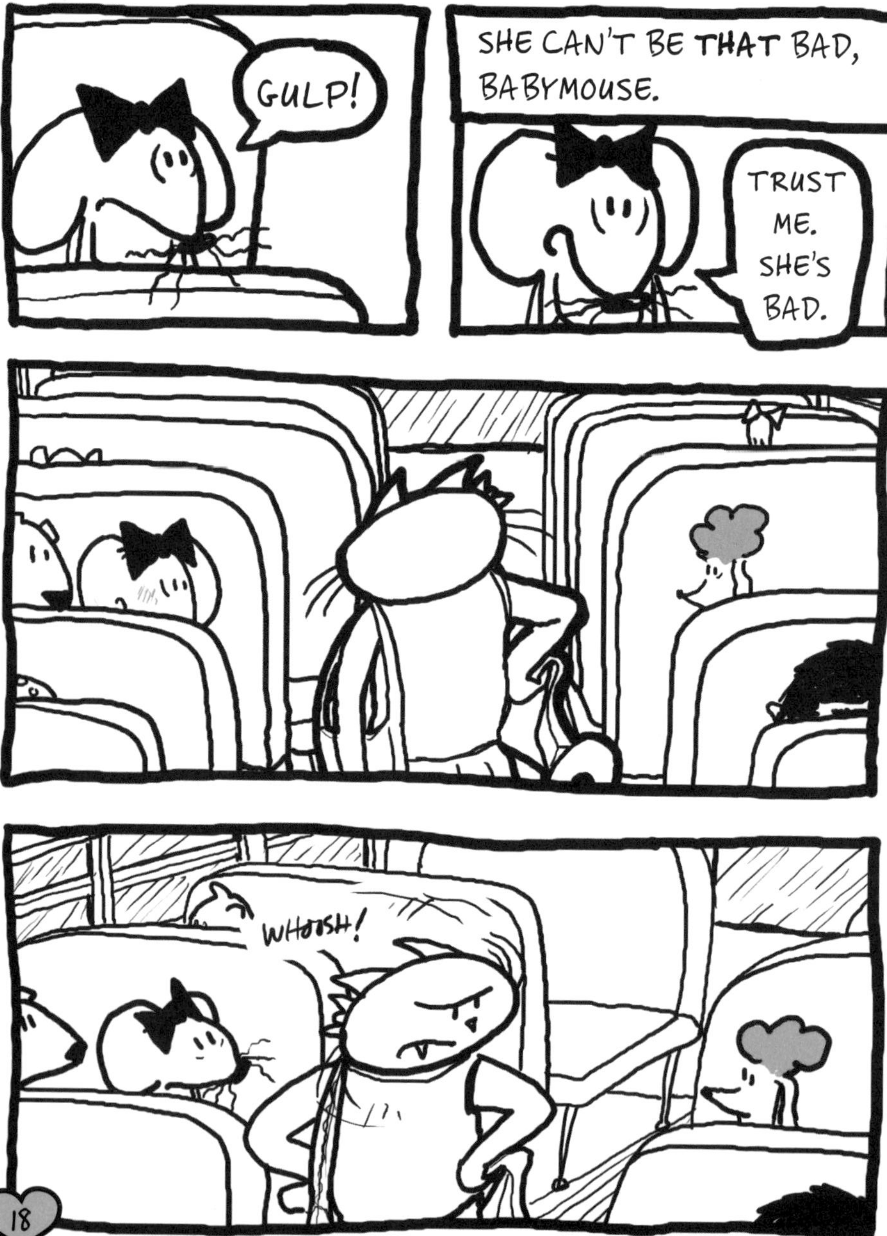

GULP!
SHE CAN'T BE **THAT** BAD, BABYMOUSE.
TRUST ME. SHE'S BAD.
WHOOSH!

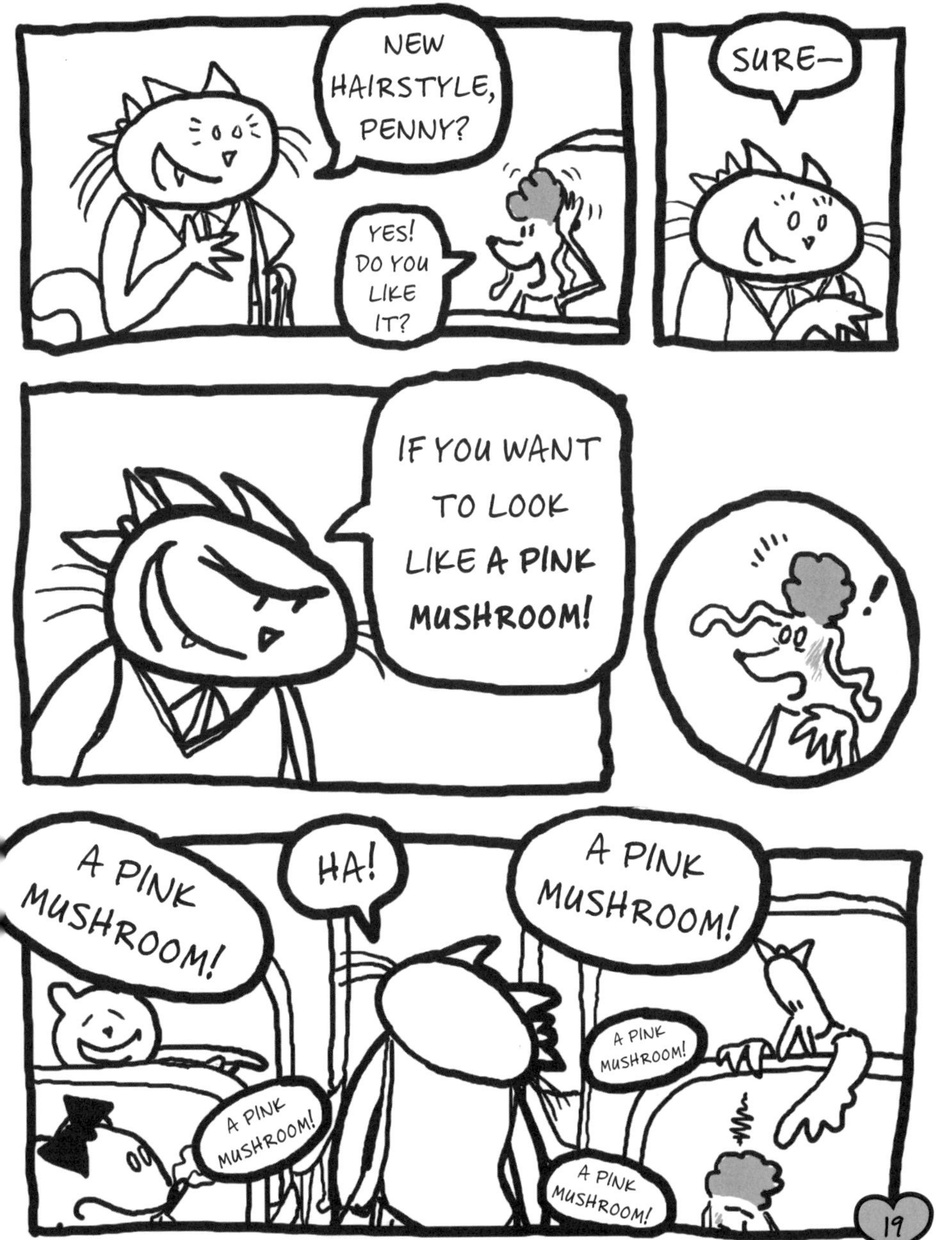
NEW HAIRSTYLE, PENNY?
YES! DO YOU LIKE IT?
SURE—
IF YOU WANT TO LOOK LIKE A **PINK MUSHROOM!**
!
A PINK MUSHROOM!
HA!
A PINK MUSHROOM!
A PINK MUSHROOM!
A PINK MUSHROOM!
A PINK MUSHROOM!

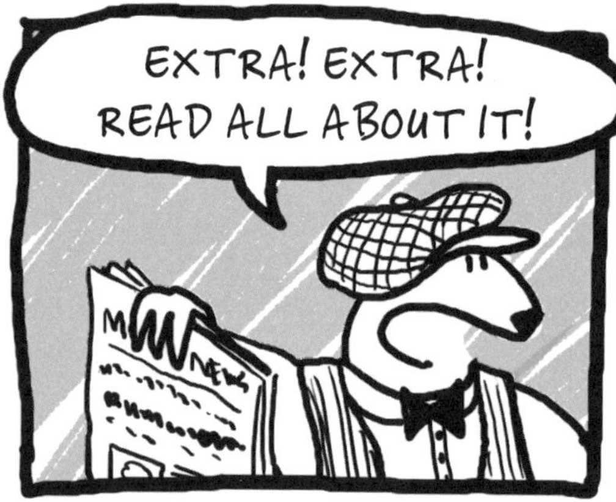
EXTRA! EXTRA! READ ALL ABOUT IT!

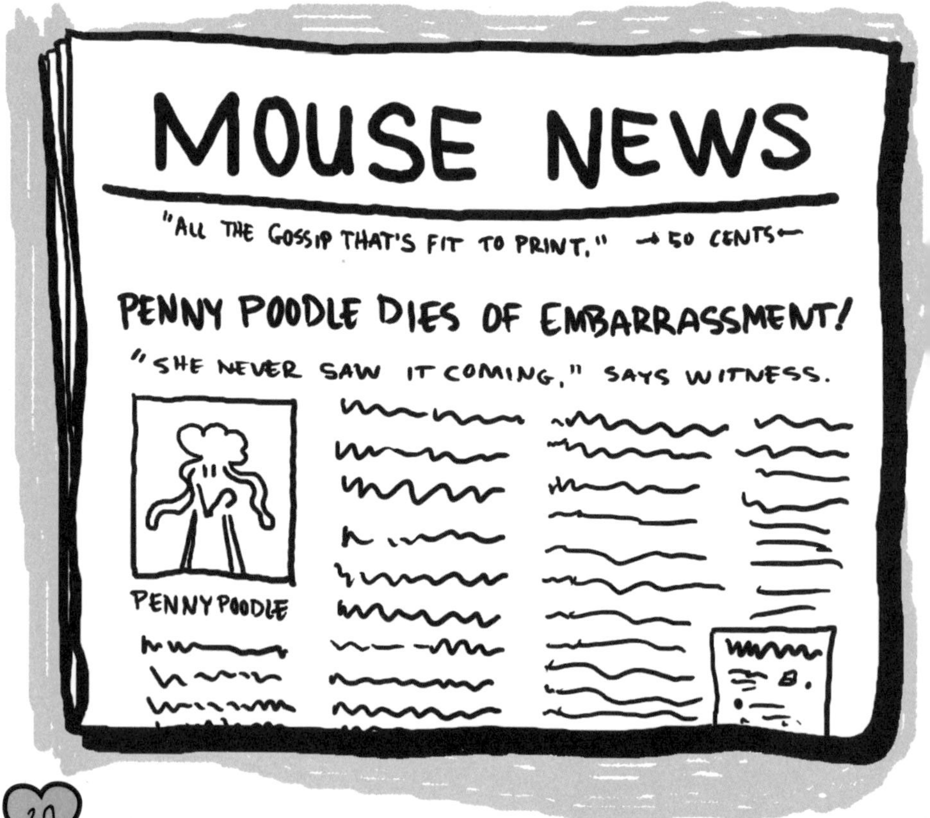
MOUSE NEWS
"ALL THE GOSSIP THAT'S FIT TO PRINT." →50 CENTS←
PENNY POODLE DIES OF EMBARRASSMENT!
"SHE NEVER SAW IT COMING," SAYS WITNESS.
PENNY POODLE

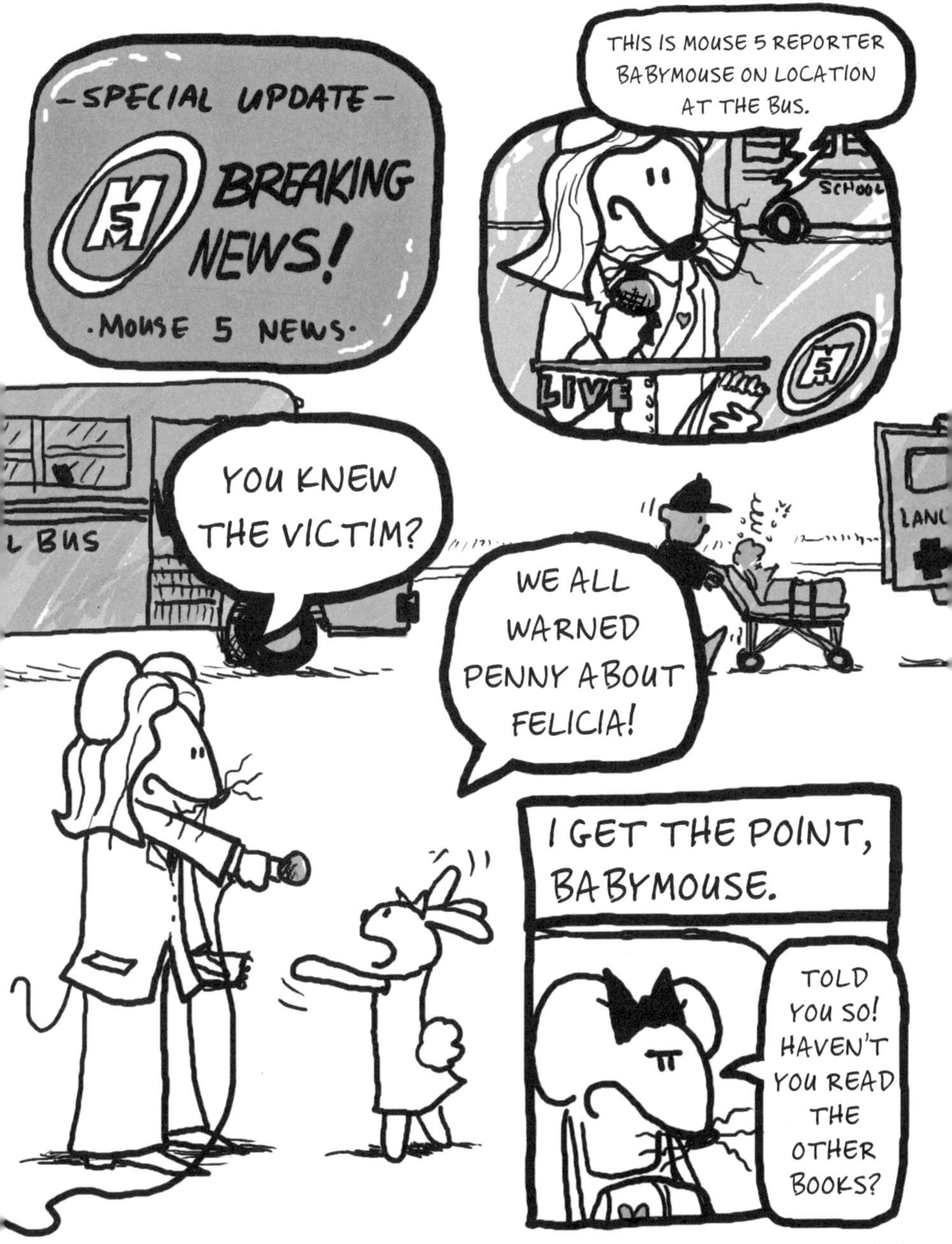
-SPECIAL UPDATE-
BREAKING NEWS!
·MOUSE 5 NEWS·
THIS IS MOUSE 5 REPORTER BABYMOUSE ON LOCATION AT THE BUS.
SCHOOL
LIVE
YOU KNEW THE VICTIM?
WE ALL WARNED PENNY ABOUT FELICIA!
I GET THE POINT, BABYMOUSE.
TOLD YOU SO! HAVEN'T YOU READ THE OTHER BOOKS?

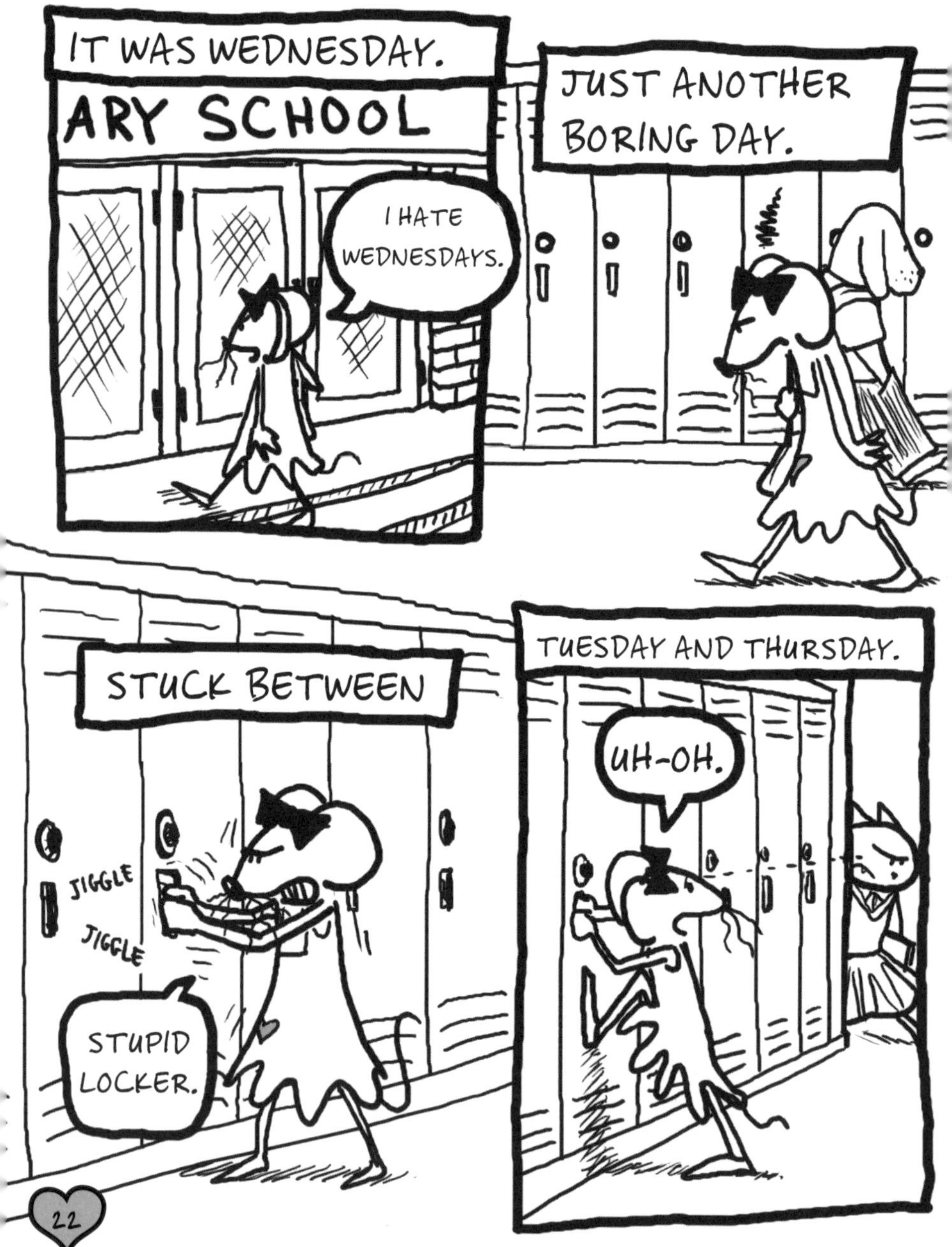
IT WAS WEDNESDAY.
ARY SCHOOL
I HATE WEDNESDAYS.
JUST ANOTHER BORING DAY.
STUCK BETWEEN
JIGGLE
JIGGLE
STUPID LOCKER.
TUESDAY AND THURSDAY.
UH-OH.

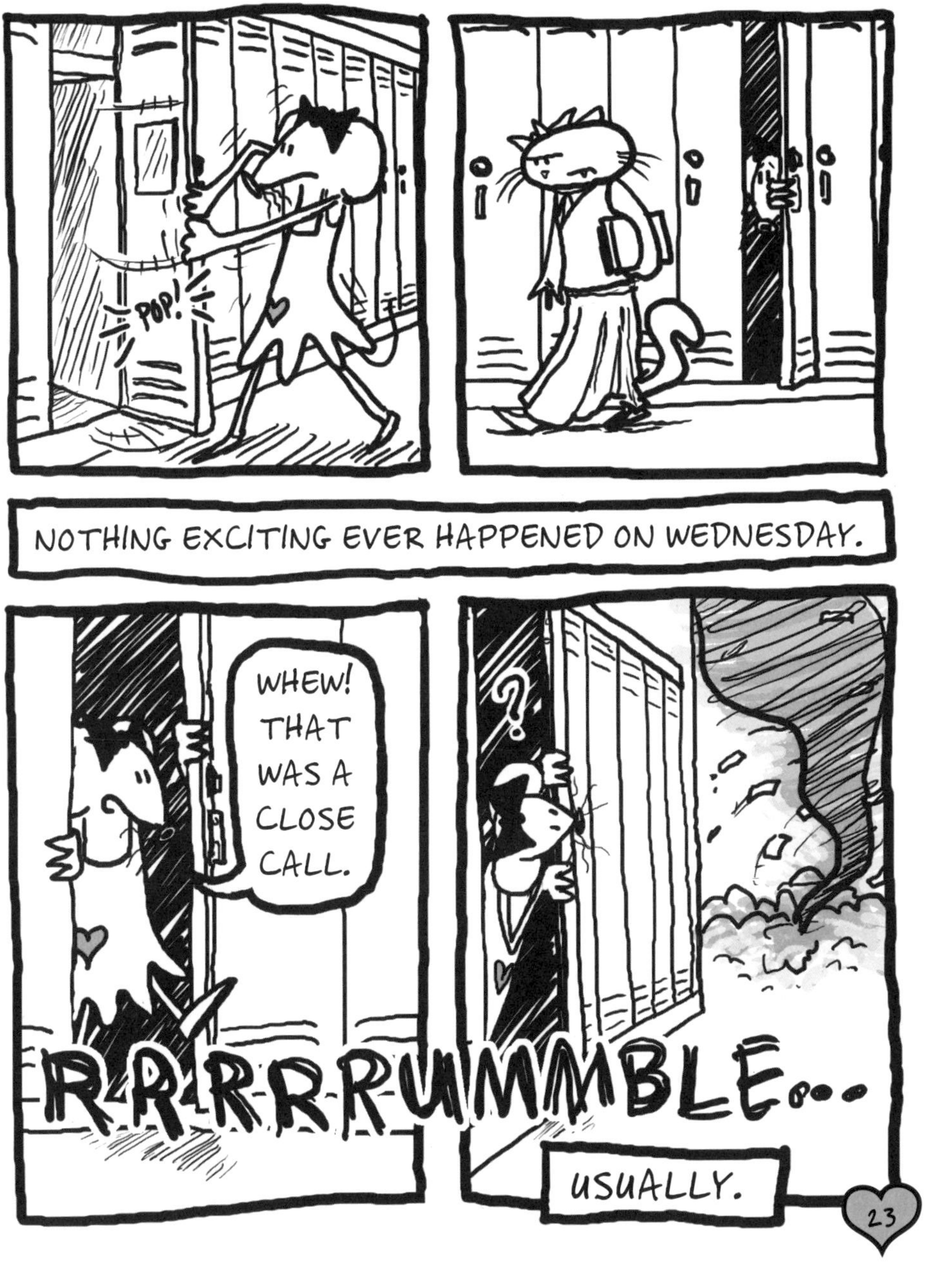
POP!
NOTHING EXCITING EVER HAPPENED ON WEDNESDAY.
WHEW! THAT WAS A CLOSE CALL.
?
RRRRRUMMBLE...
USUALLY.

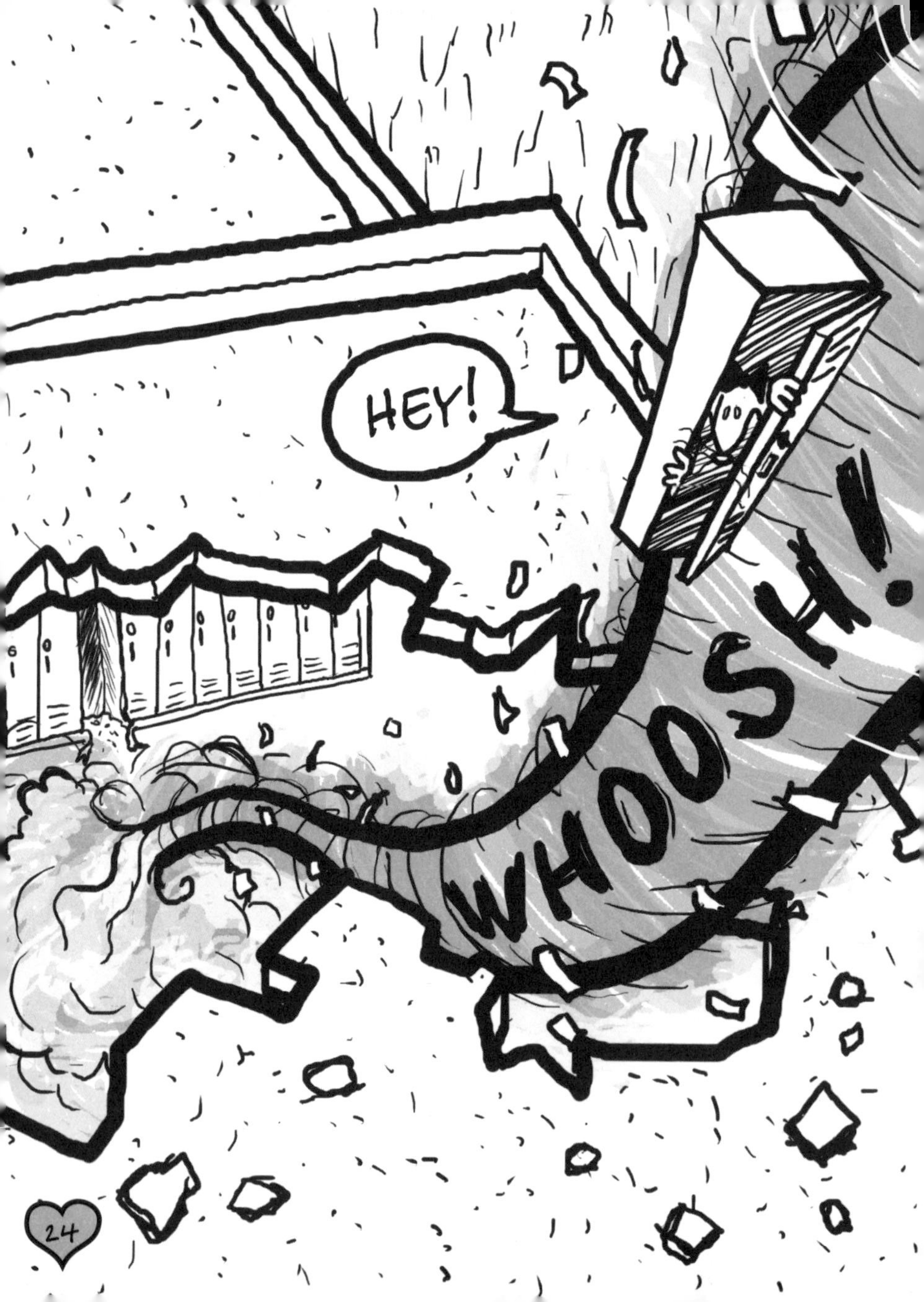
HEY!
WHOOSH!

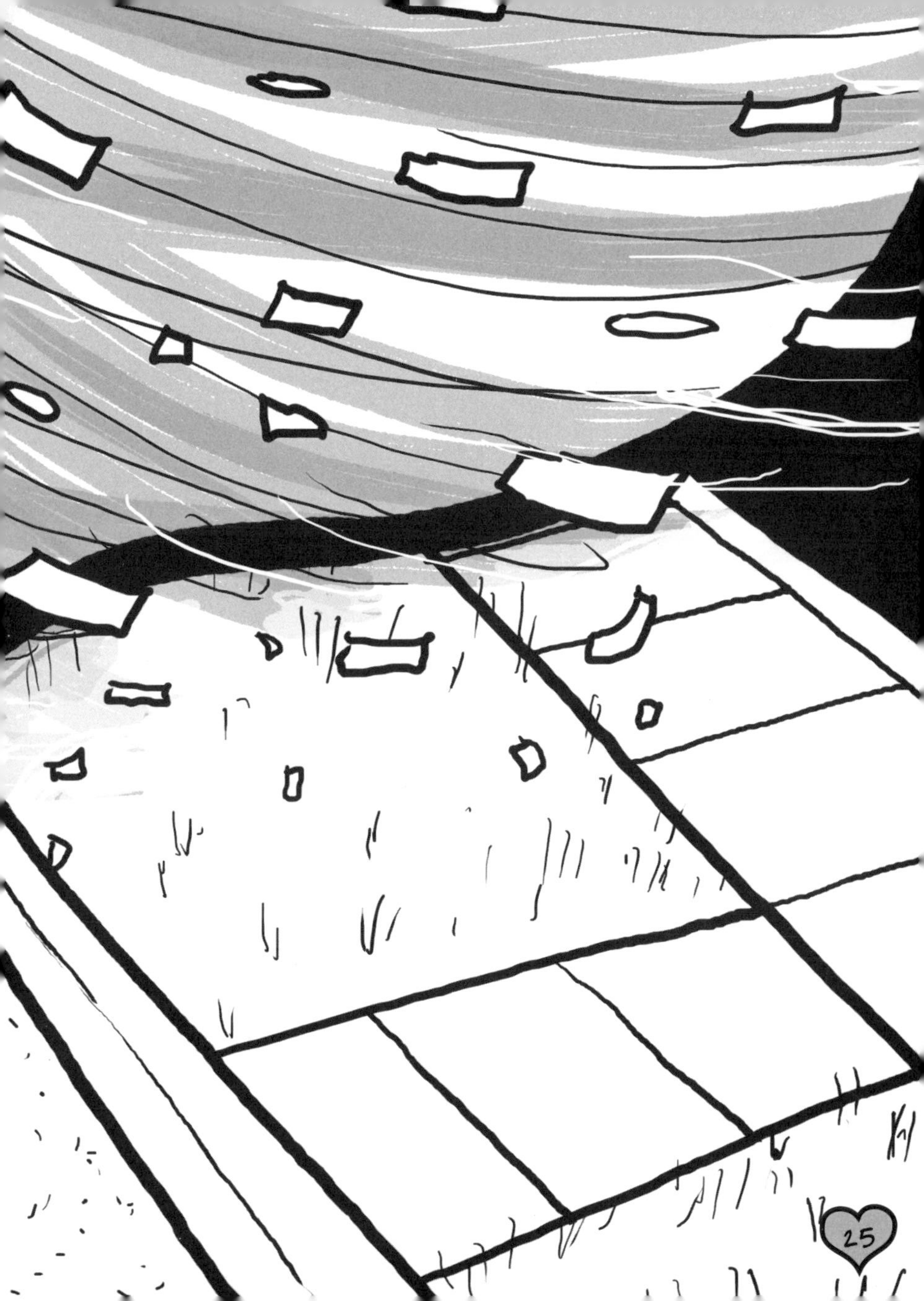

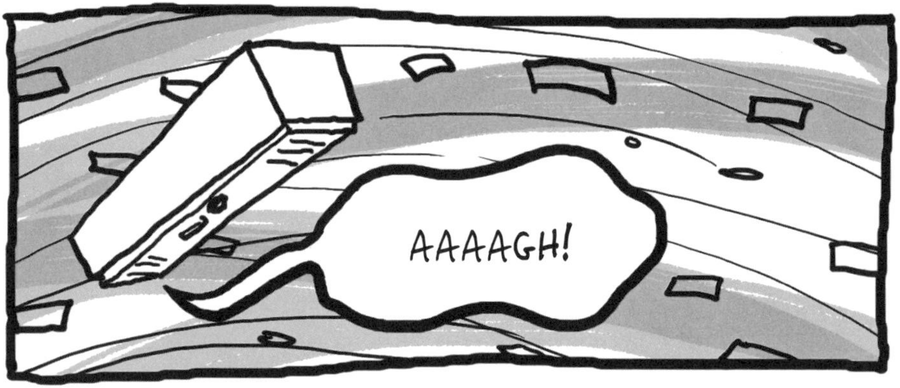
AAAAGH!

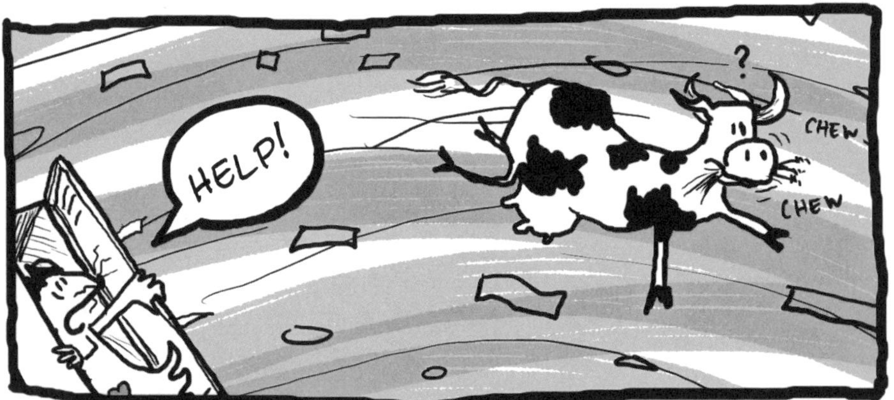
HELP!
?
CHEW
CHEW

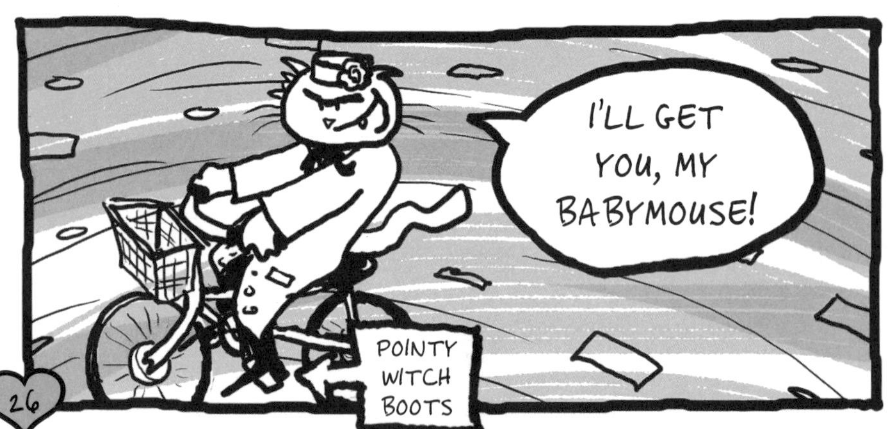
I'LL GET YOU, MY BABYMOUSE!
POINTY WITCH BOOTS

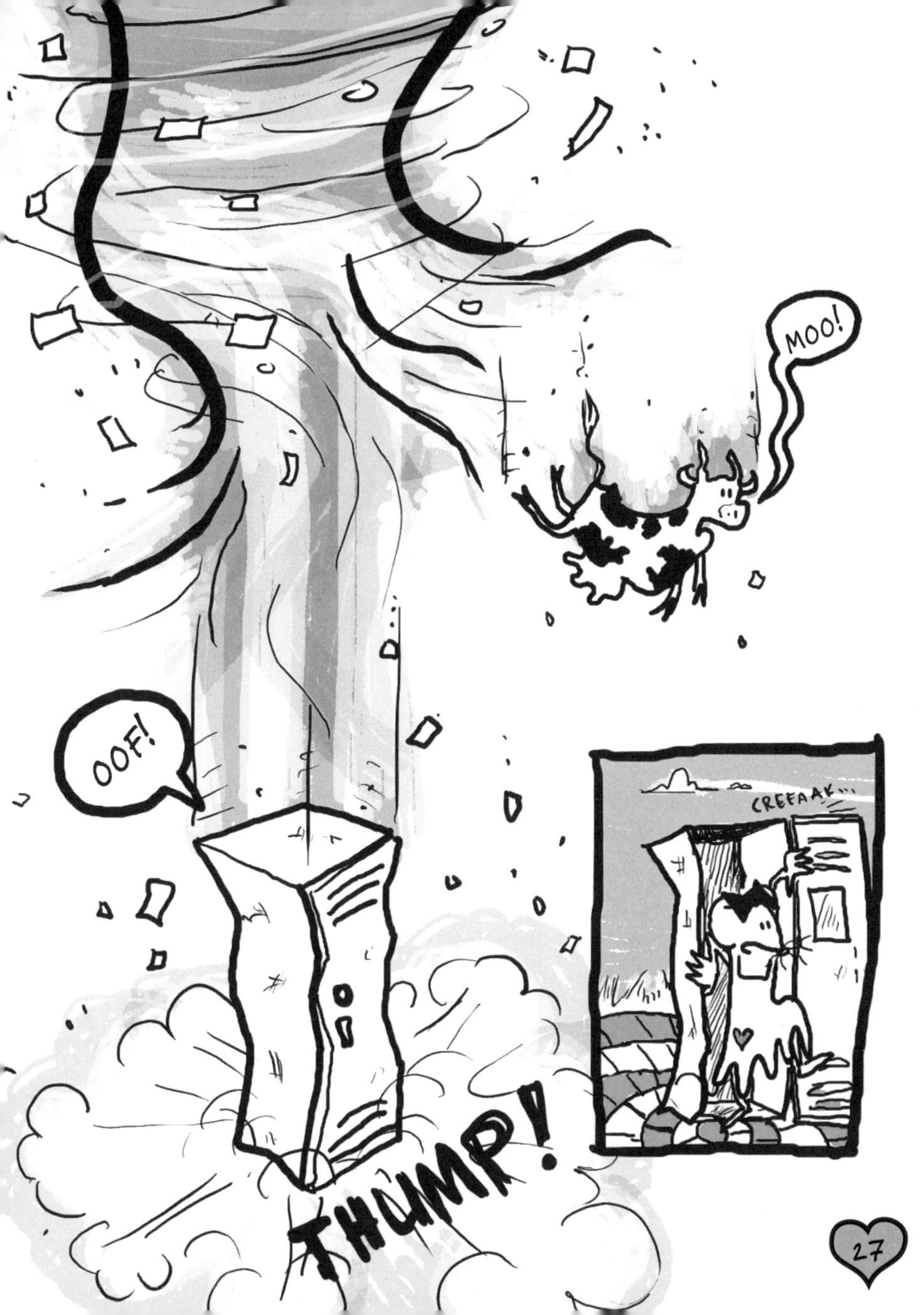
MOO!
OOF!
THUMP!
CREEAAK...

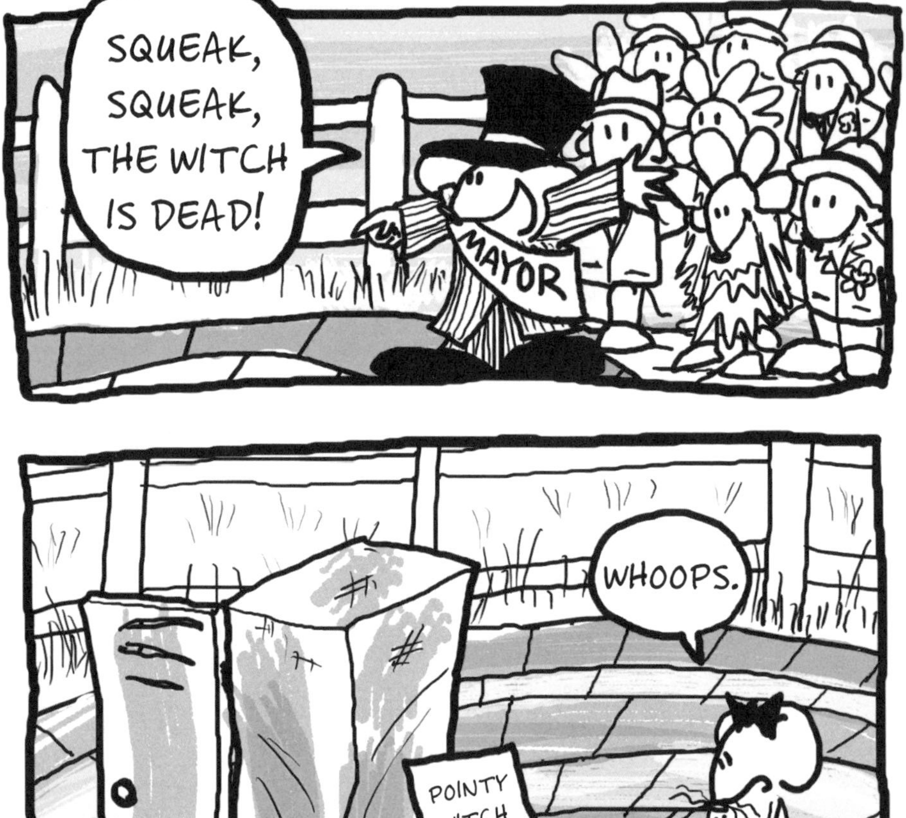
SQUEAK, SQUEAK, THE WITCH IS DEAD!
MAYOR
WHOOPS.
POINTY WITCH BOOTS
DEAD WITCH!
YOU KNOW WHO!

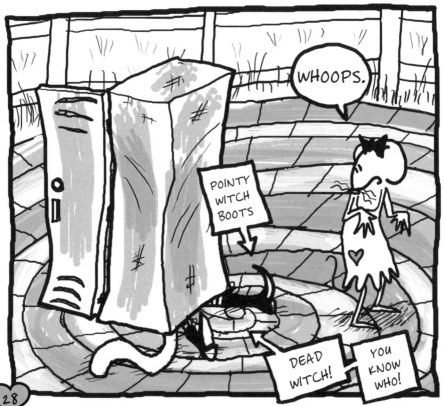

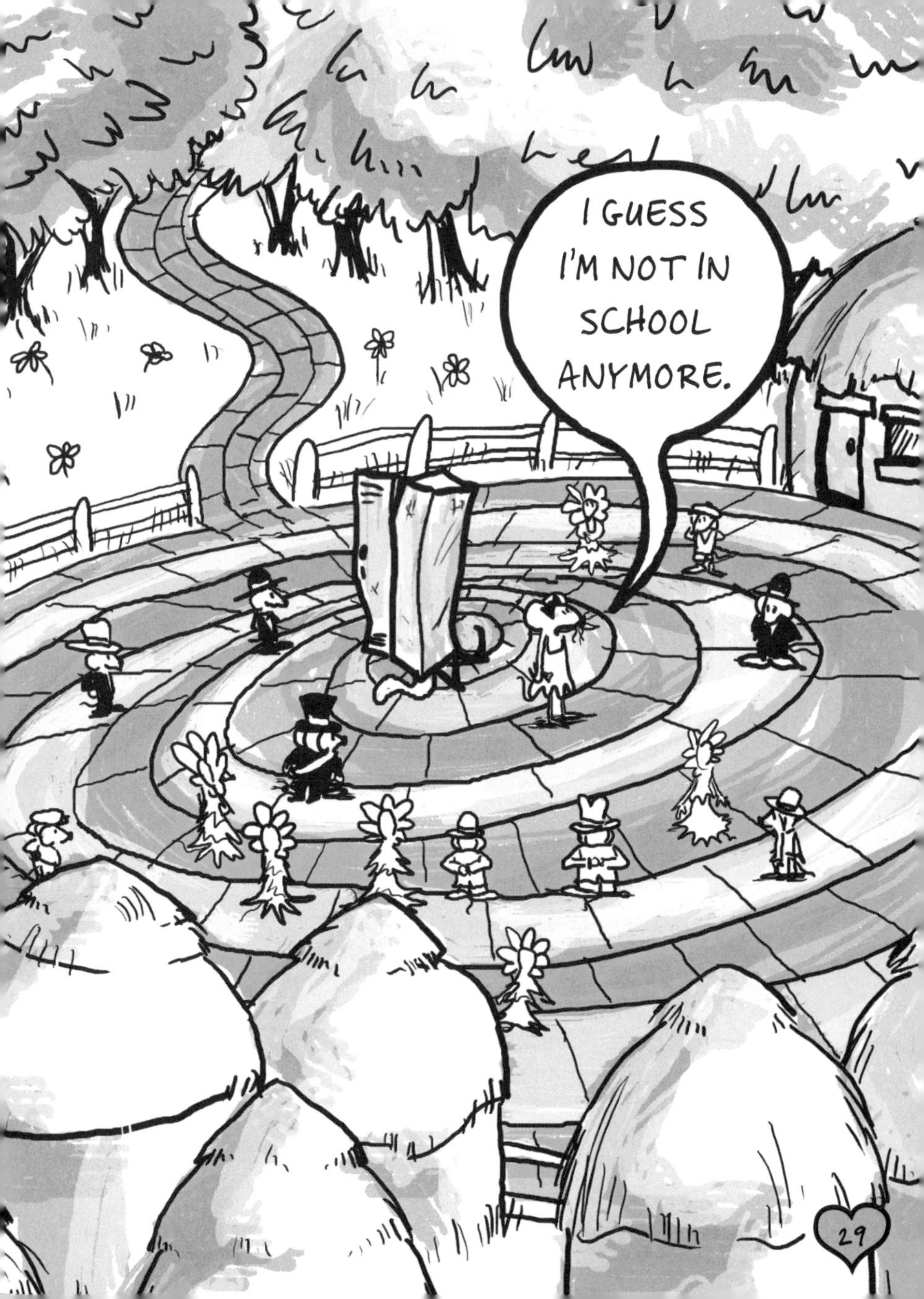
I GUESS I'M NOT IN SCHOOL ANYMORE.

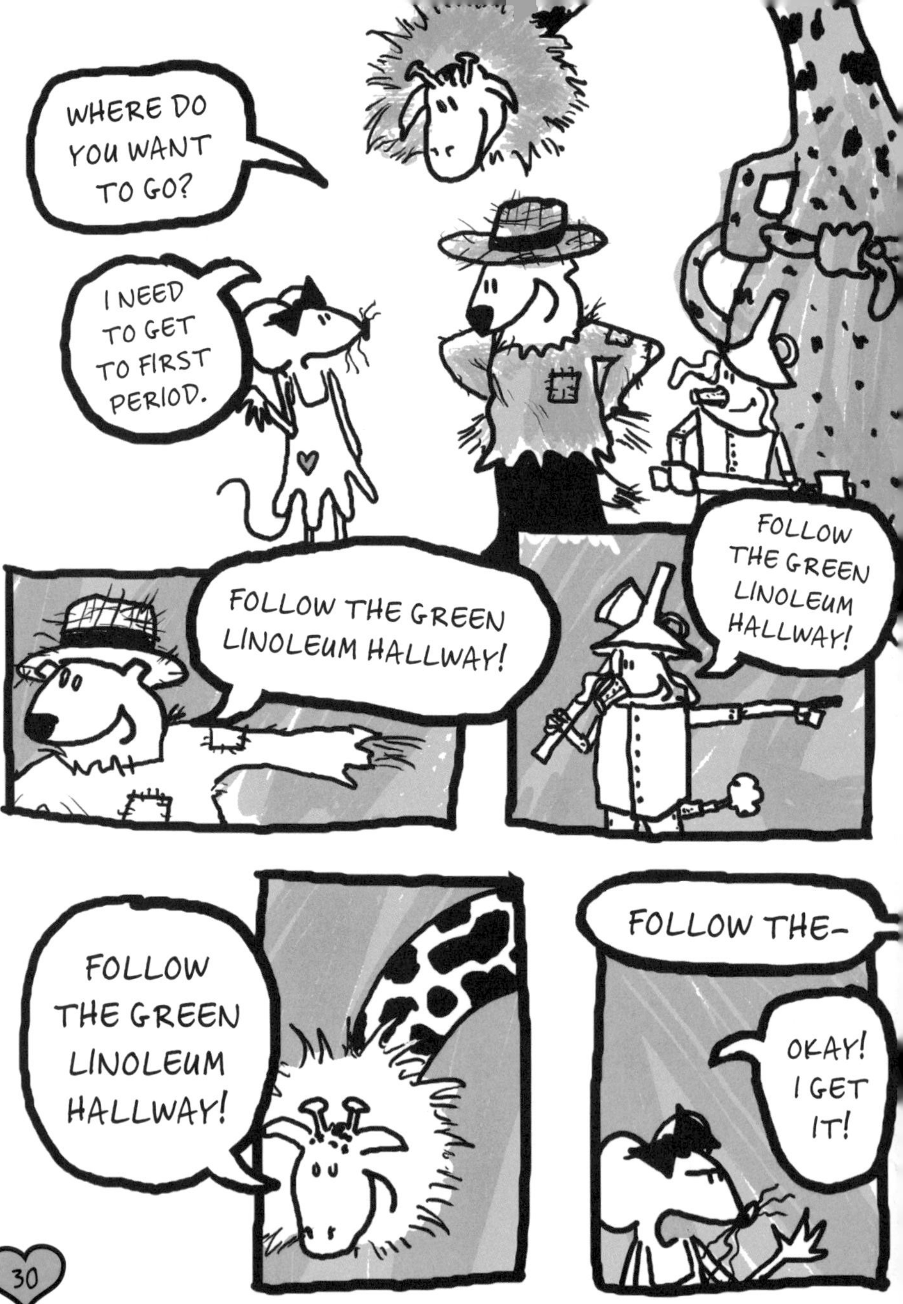
WHERE DO YOU WANT TO GO?
I NEED TO GET TO FIRST PERIOD.
FOLLOW THE GREEN LINOLEUM HALLWAY!
FOLLOW THE GREEN LINOLEUM HALLWAY!
FOLLOW THE GREEN LINOLEUM HALLWAY!
FOLLOW THE-
OKAY! I GET IT!

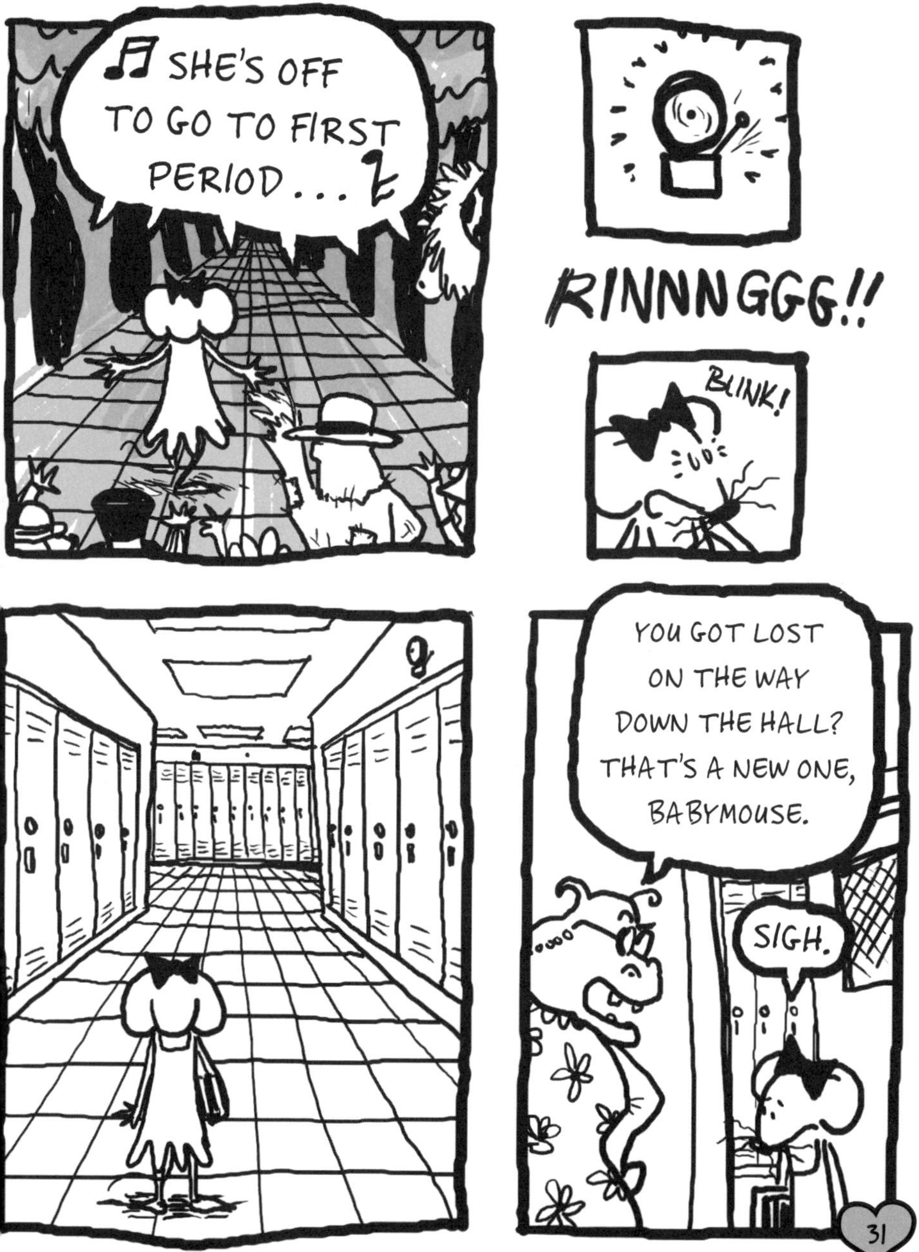
♫ SHE'S OFF TO GO TO FIRST PERIOD...
RINNNGGG!!
BLINK!
YOU GOT LOST ON THE WAY DOWN THE HALL? THAT'S A NEW ONE, BABYMOUSE.
SIGH.

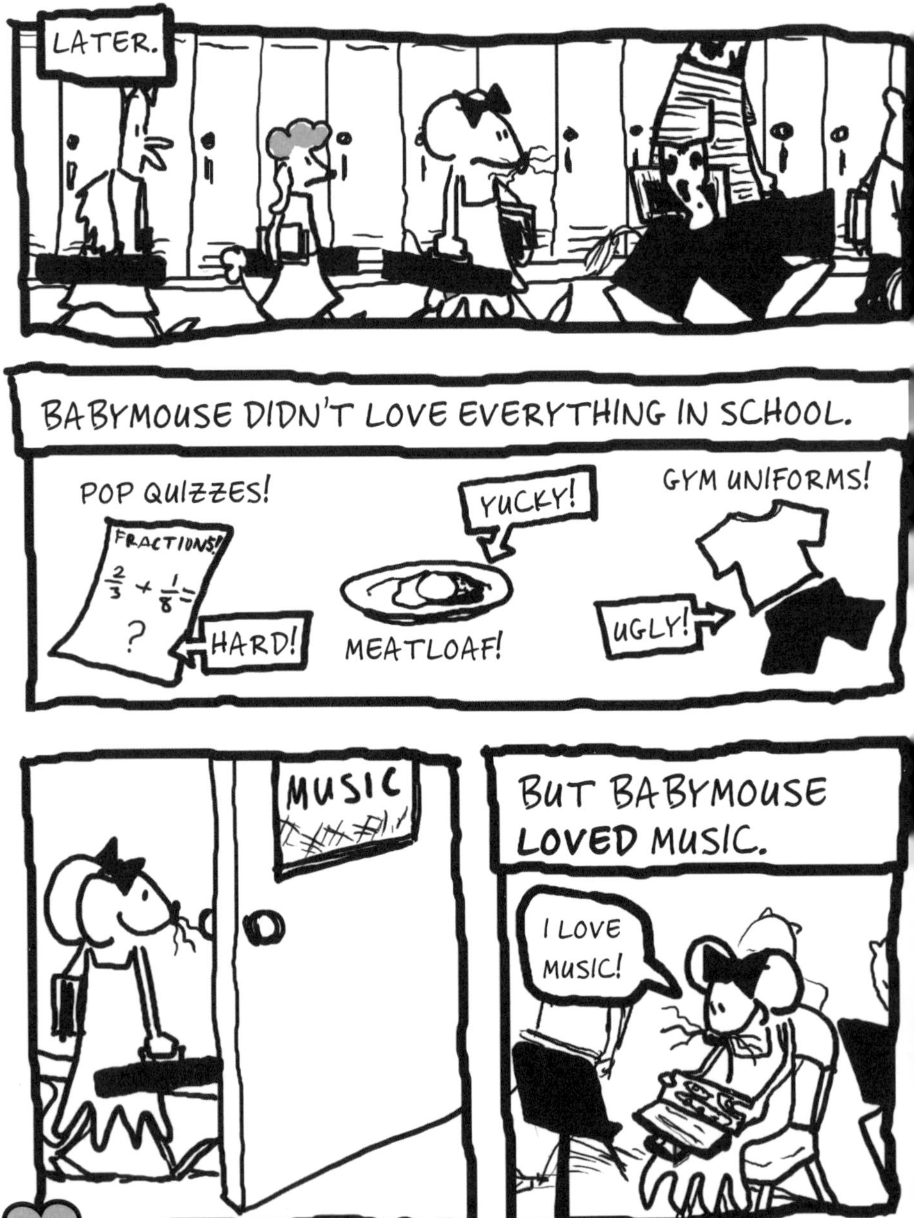
LATER.
BABYMOUSE DIDN'T LOVE EVERYTHING IN SCHOOL.
POP QUIZZES!
FRACTIONS!
2/3 + 1/8 =
?
HARD!
YUCKY!
MEATLOAF!
GYM UNIFORMS!
UGLY!
MUSIC
BUT BABYMOUSE **LOVED** MUSIC.
I LOVE MUSIC!

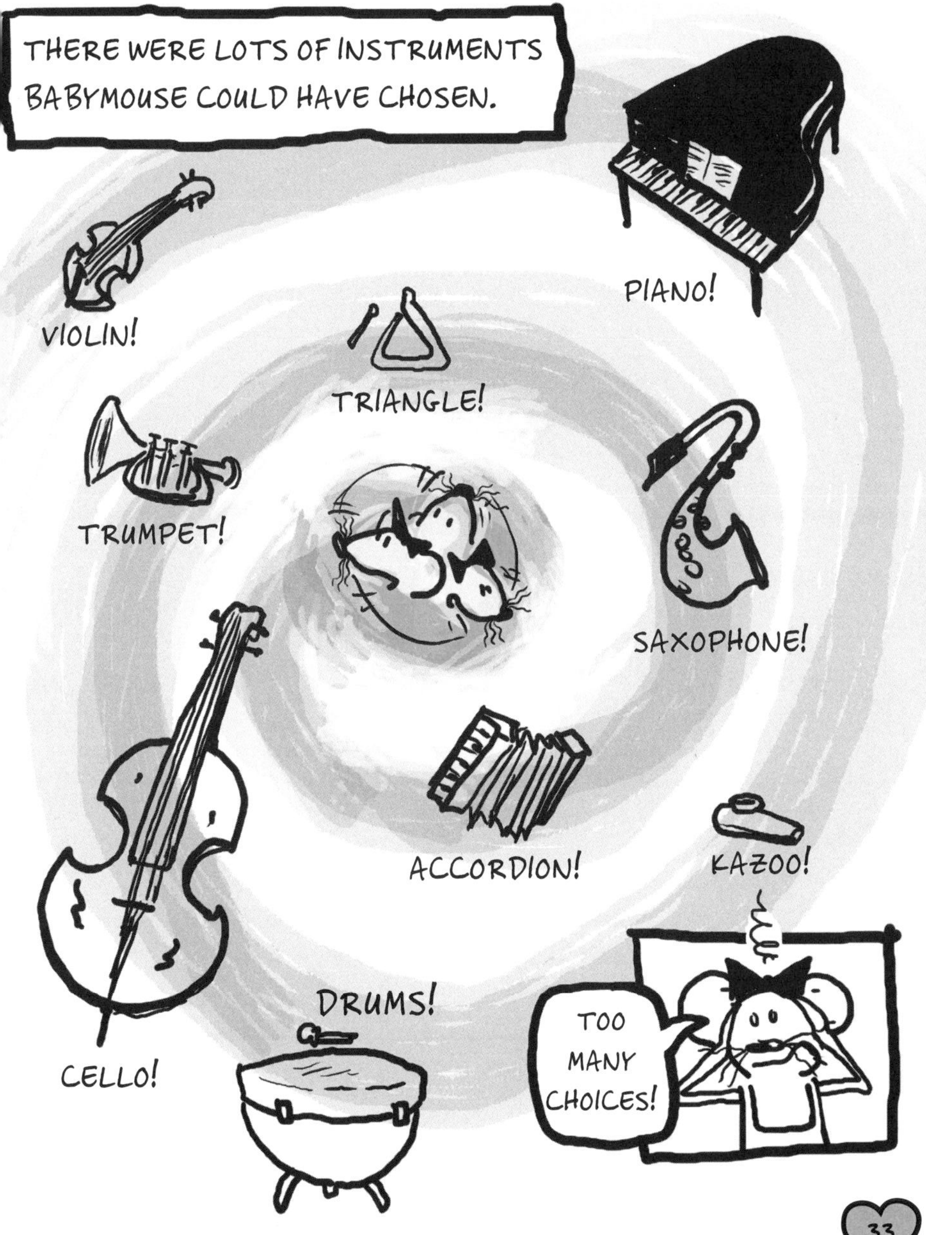
THERE WERE LOTS OF INSTRUMENTS BABYMOUSE COULD HAVE CHOSEN.
PIANO!
VIOLIN!
TRIANGLE!
TRUMPET!
SAXOPHONE!
ACCORDION!
KAZOO!
DRUMS!
CELLO!
TOO MANY CHOICES!

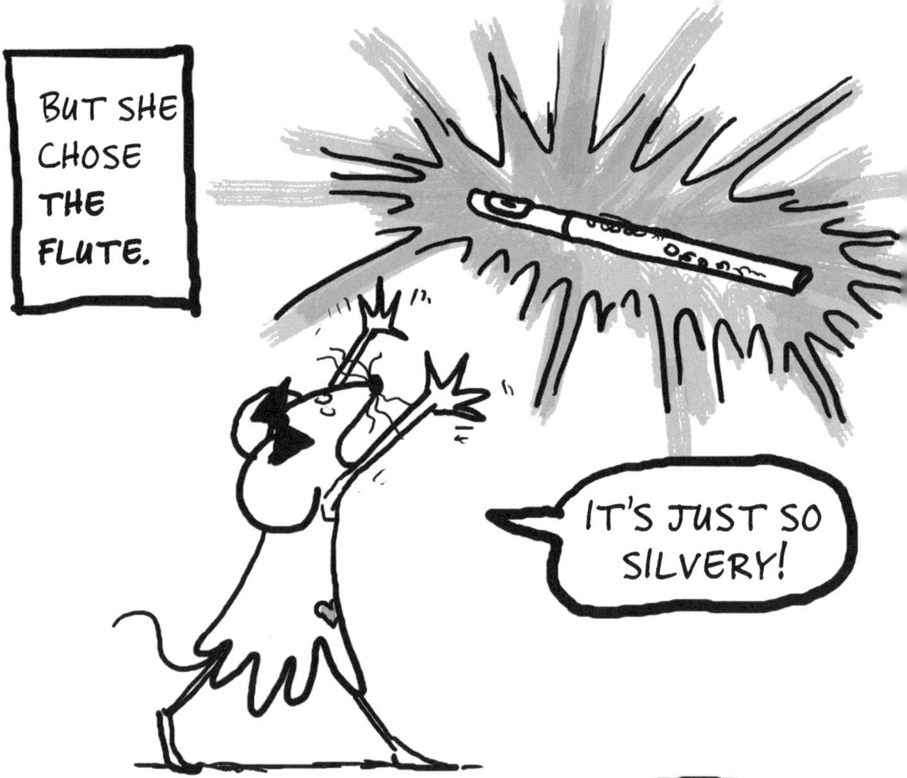
BUT SHE CHOSE THE FLUTE.
IT'S JUST SO SILVERY!

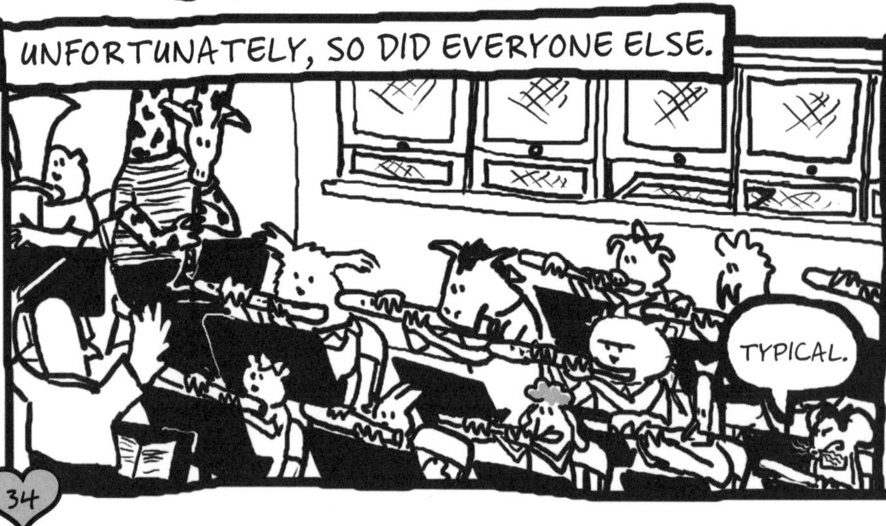
UNFORTUNATELY, SO DID EVERYONE ELSE.
TYPICAL.

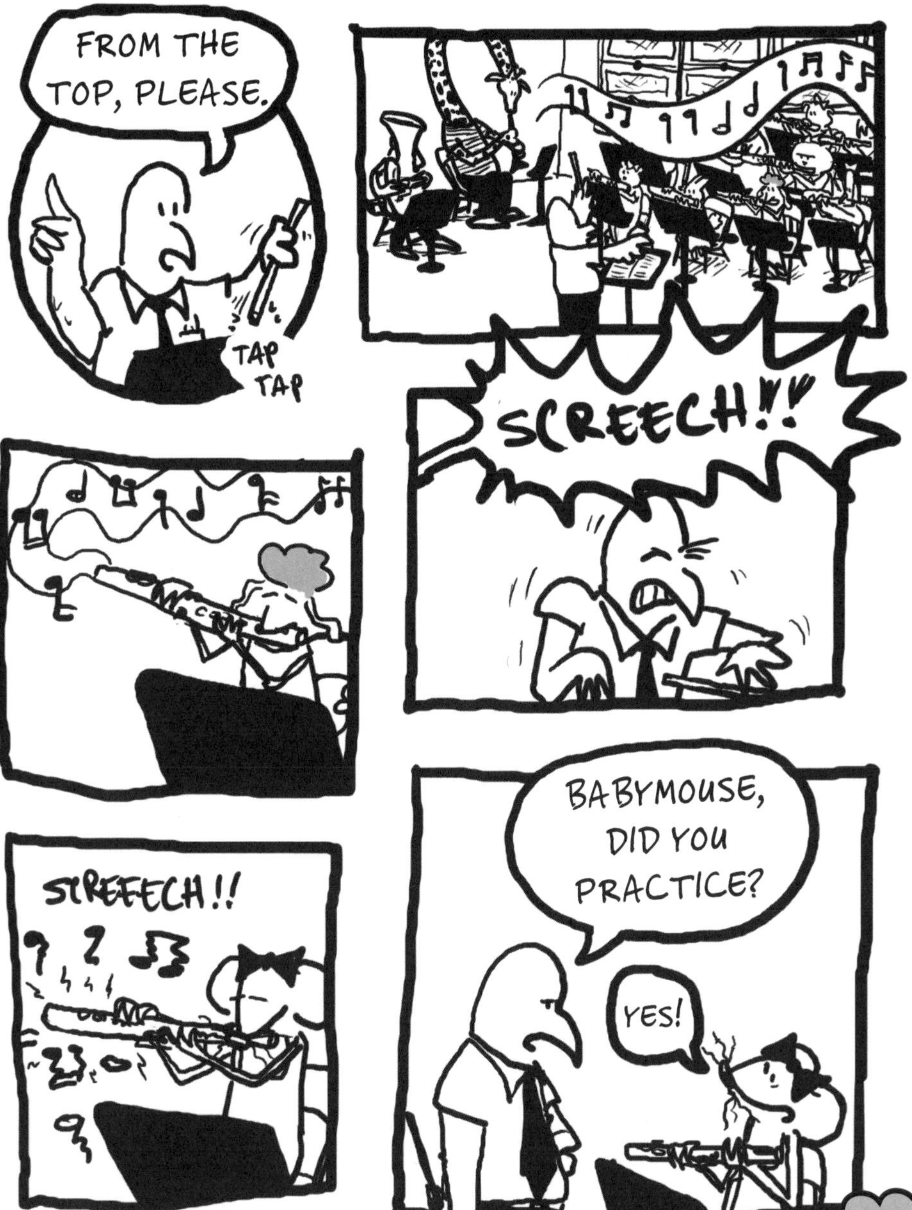
FROM THE TOP, PLEASE.
TAP TAP
SCREECH!!!
SCREEECH!!
BABYMOUSE, DID YOU PRACTICE?
YES!

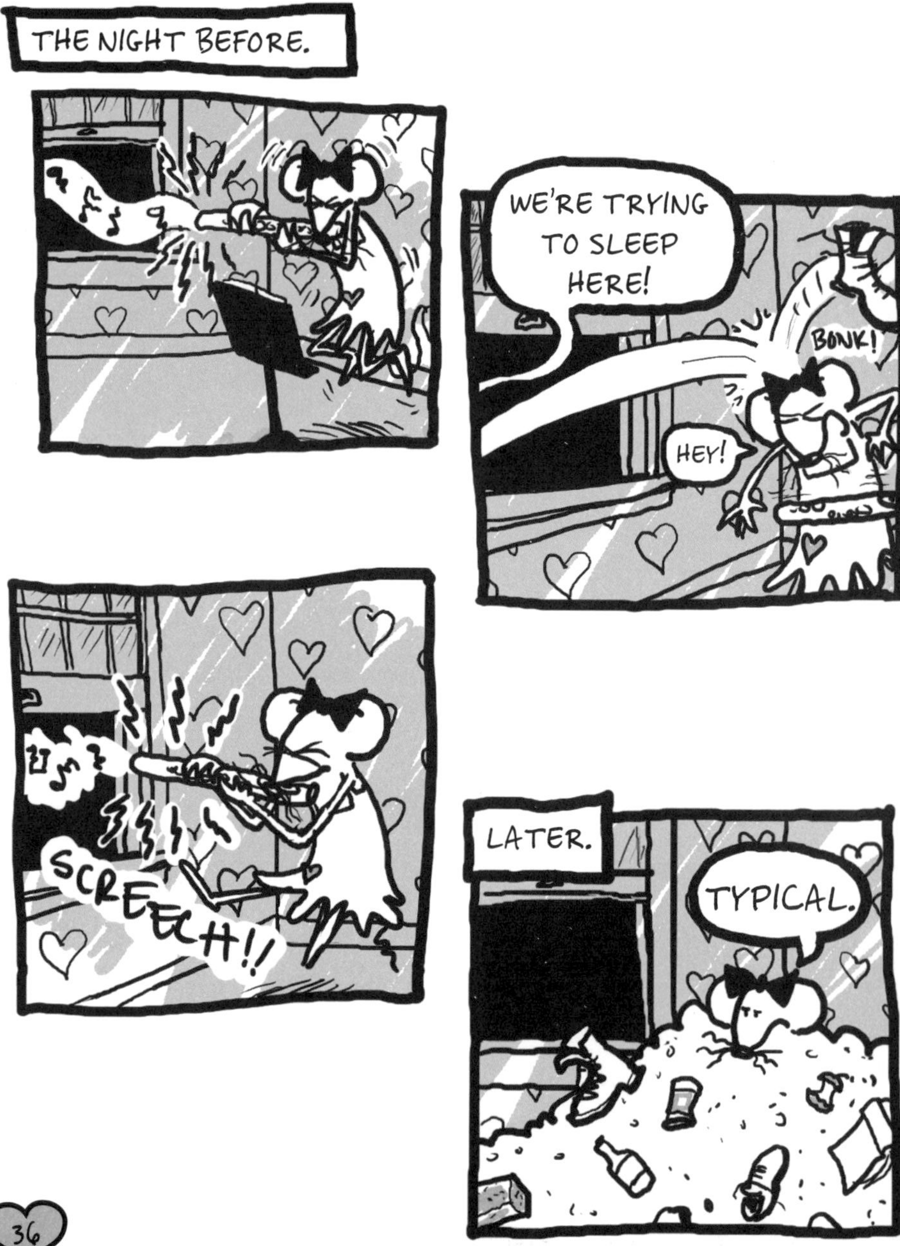
THE NIGHT BEFORE.
WE'RE TRYING TO SLEEP HERE!
BONK!
HEY!
SCREEECH!!
LATER.
TYPICAL.

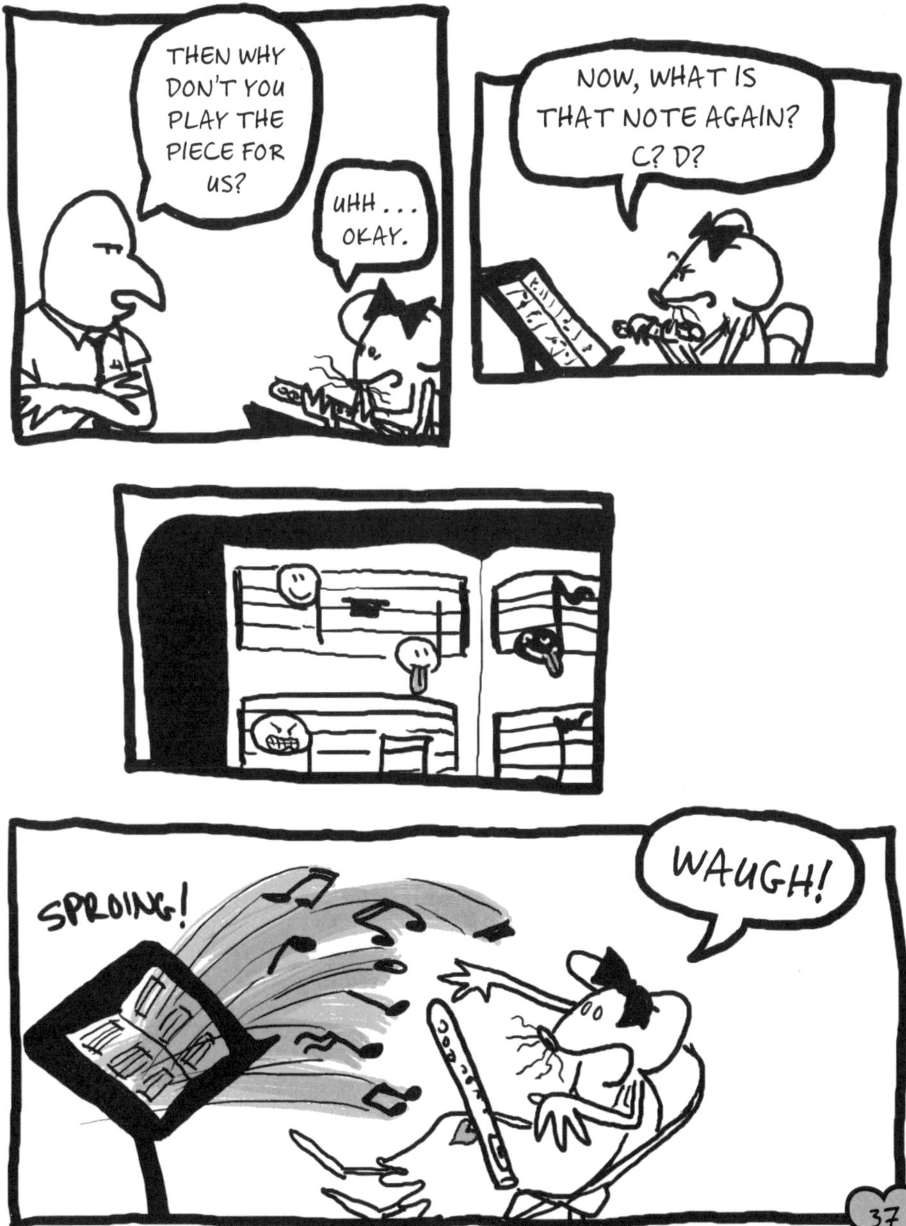
THEN WHY DON'T YOU PLAY THE PIECE FOR US?
UHH . . . OKAY.
NOW, WHAT IS THAT NOTE AGAIN? C? D?
SPROING!
WAUGH!

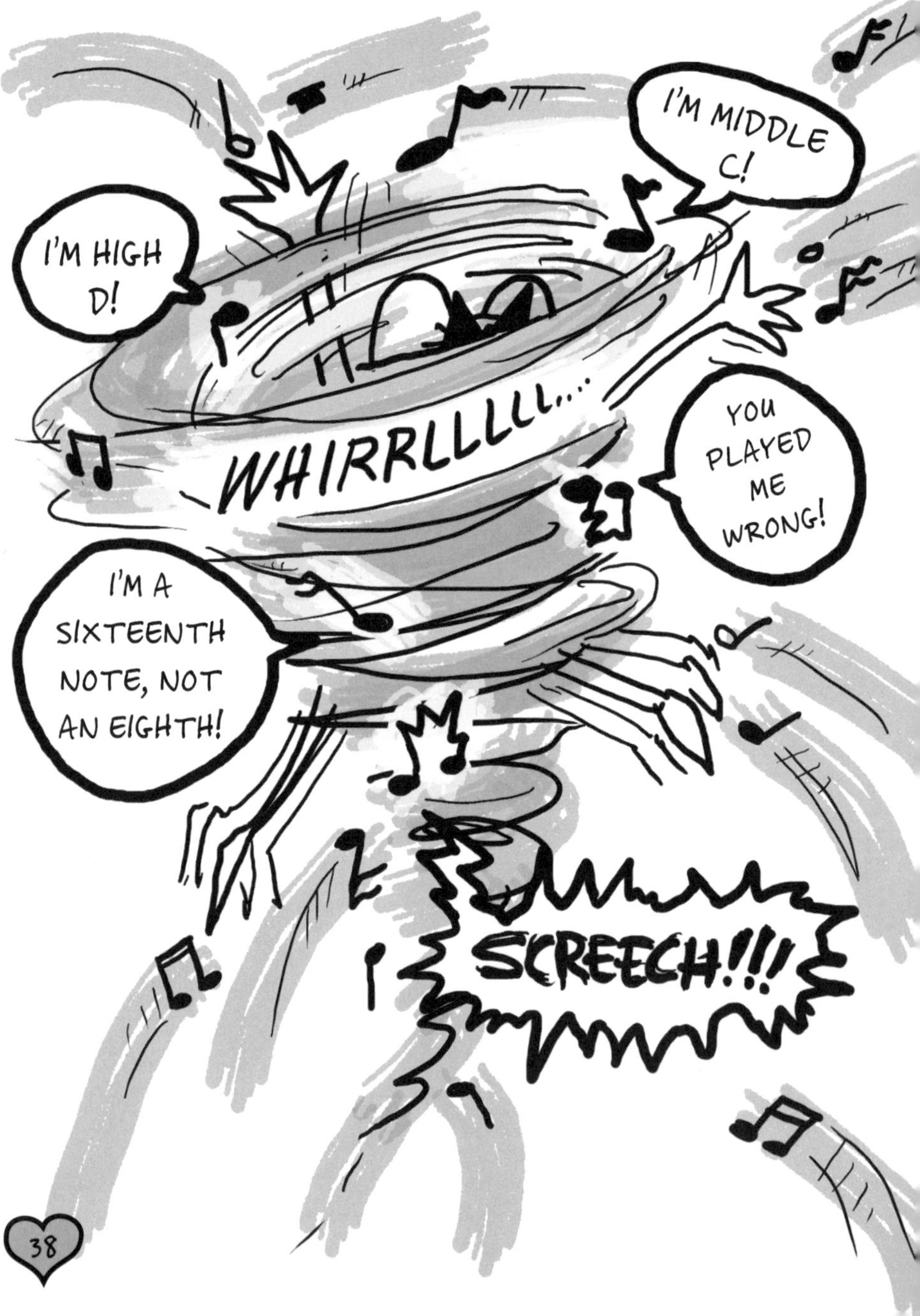
I'M MIDDLE C!
I'M HIGH D!
WHIRRLLLLL...
YOU PLAYED ME WRONG!
I'M A SIXTEENTH NOTE, NOT AN EIGHTH!
SCREECH!!!

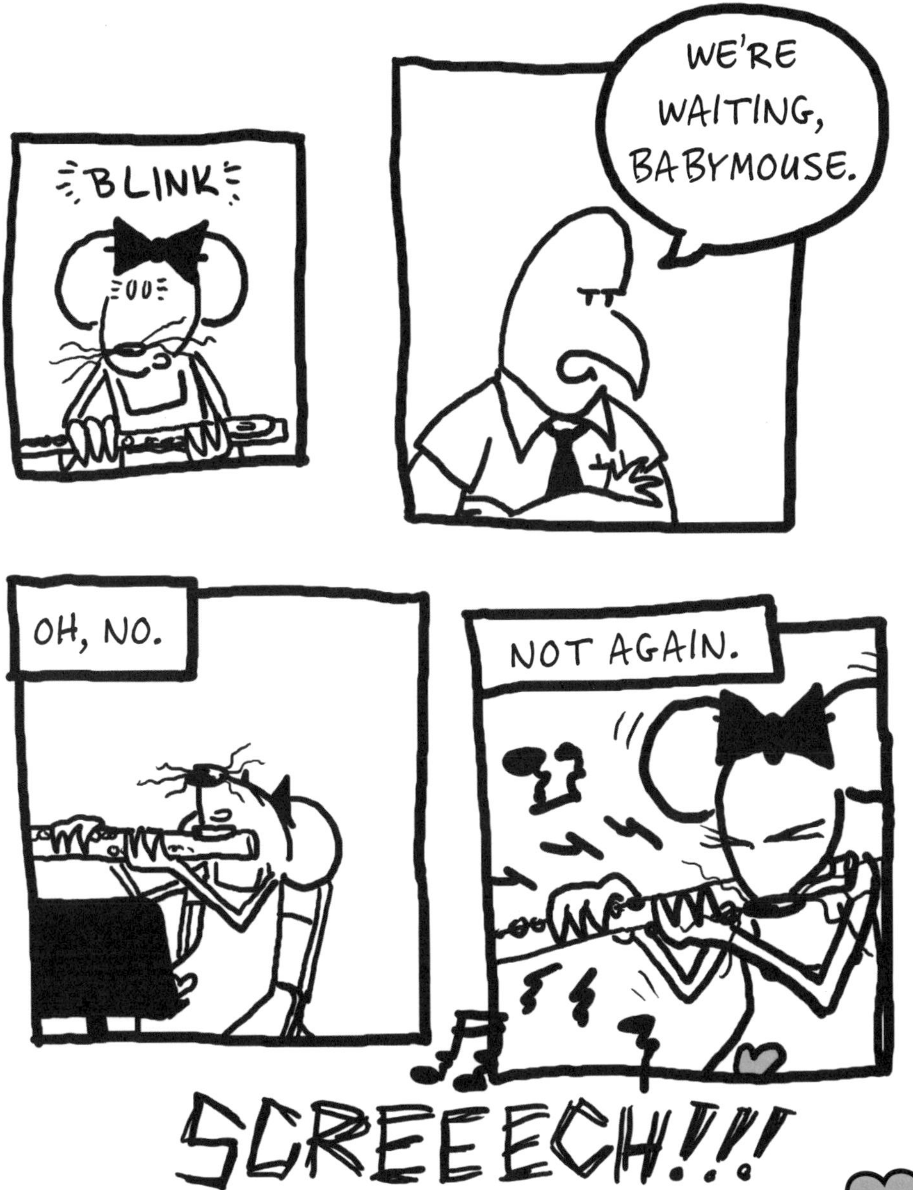
BLINK
WE'RE WAITING, BABYMOUSE.
OH, NO.
NOT AGAIN.
SCREEECH!!!

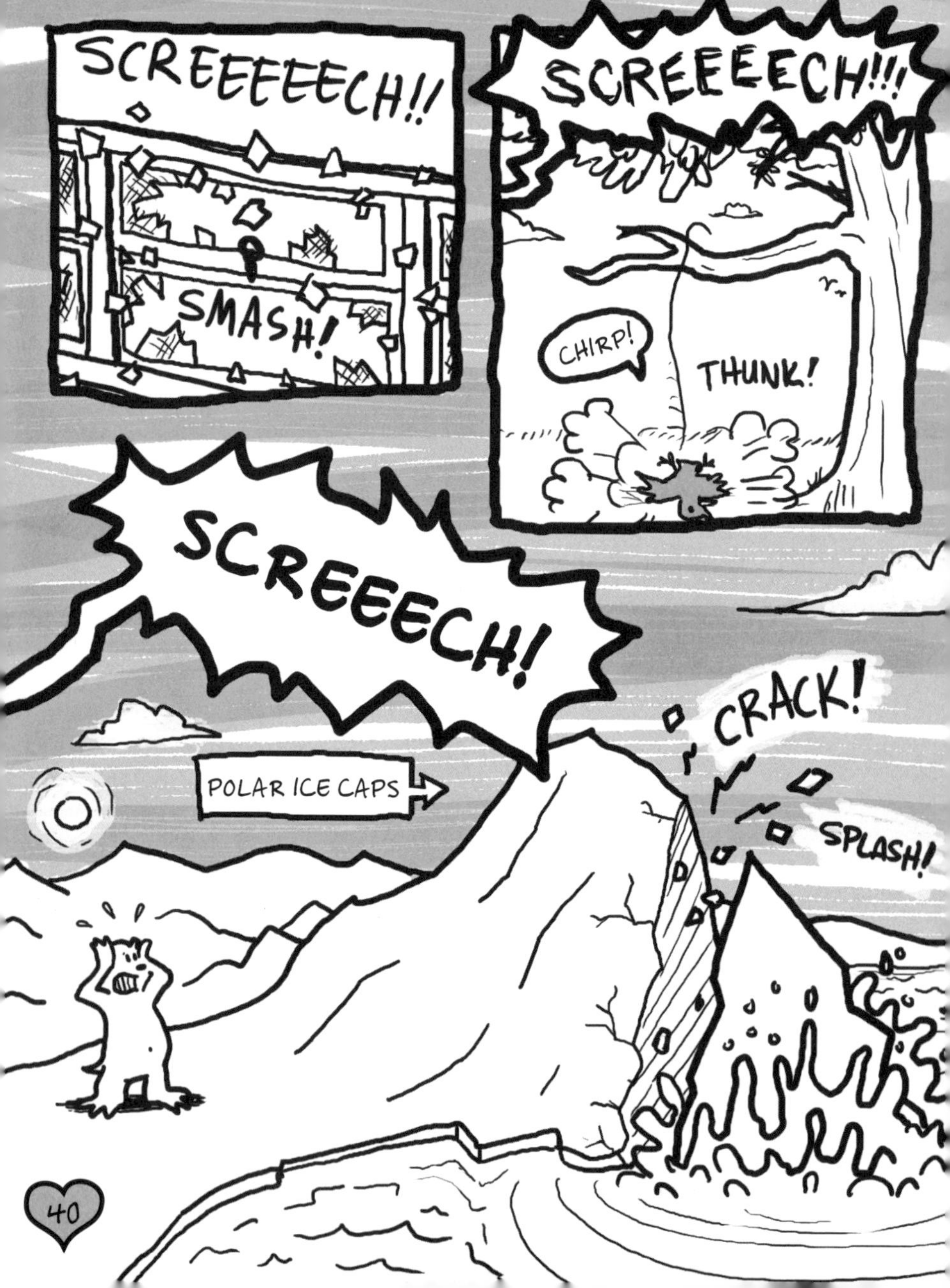
SCREEEEECH!!
SMASH!
SCREEEEECH!!!
CHIRP!
THUNK!
SCREEEECH!
POLAR ICE CAPS
CRACK!
SPLASH!

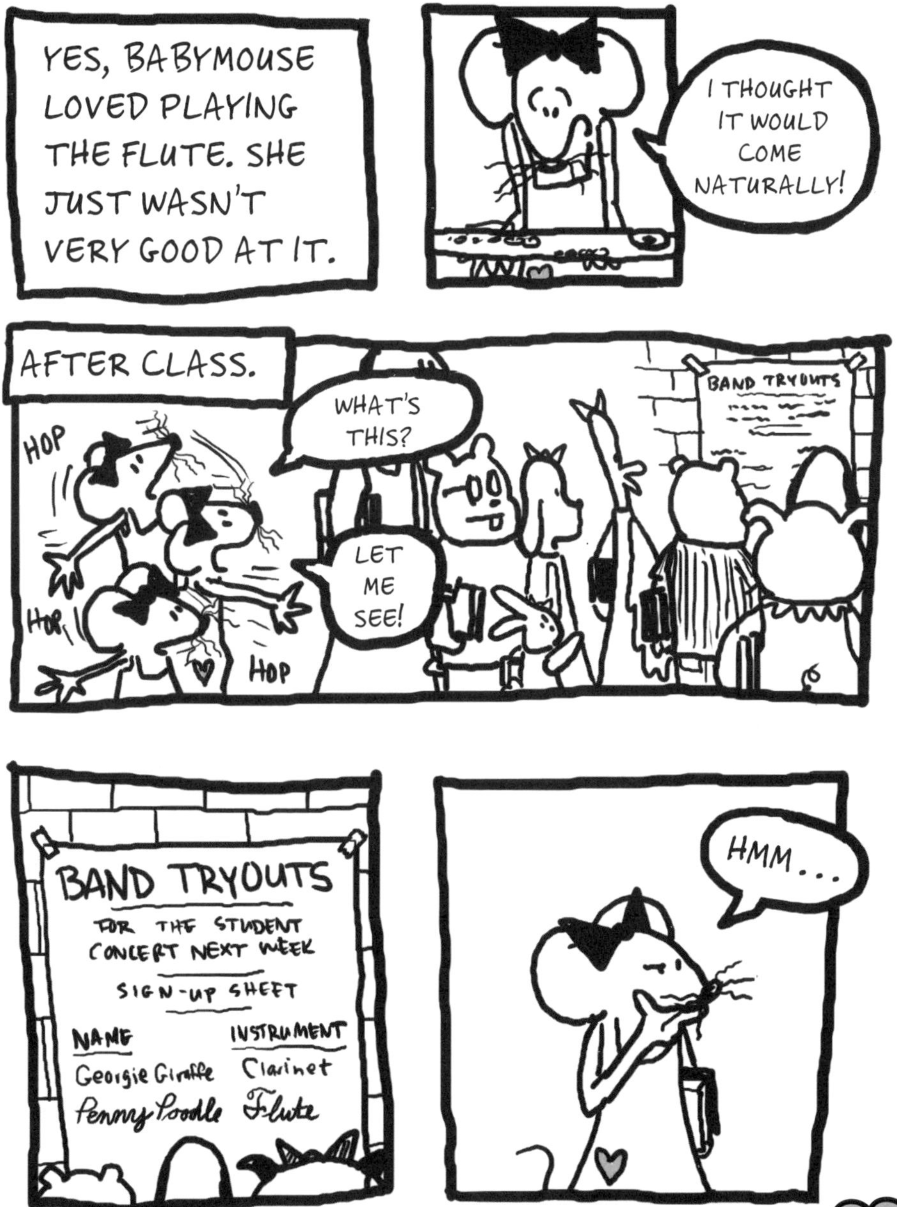
YES, BABYMOUSE LOVED PLAYING THE FLUTE. SHE JUST WASN'T VERY GOOD AT IT.
I THOUGHT IT WOULD COME NATURALLY!
AFTER CLASS.
HOP
HOP
HOP
WHAT'S THIS?
LET ME SEE!
BAND TRYOUTS
BAND TRYOUTS
FOR THE STUDENT CONCERT NEXT WEEK
SIGN-UP SHEET
NAME
INSTRUMENT
Georgie Giraffe
Clarinet
Penny Poodle
Flute
HMM...

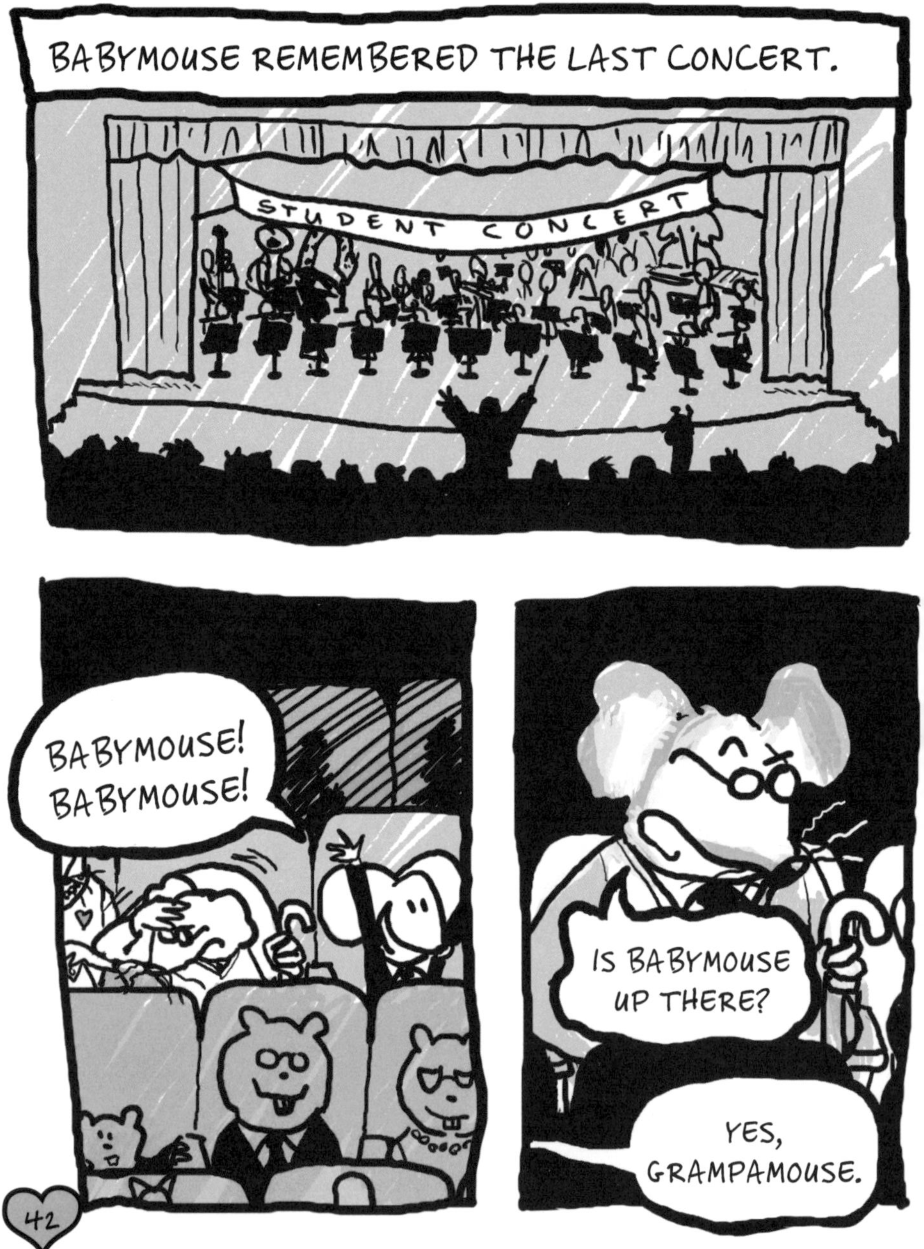
BABYMOUSE REMEMBERED THE LAST CONCERT.
STUDENT CONCERT
BABYMOUSE! BABYMOUSE!
IS BABYMOUSE UP THERE?
YES, GRAMPAMOUSE.

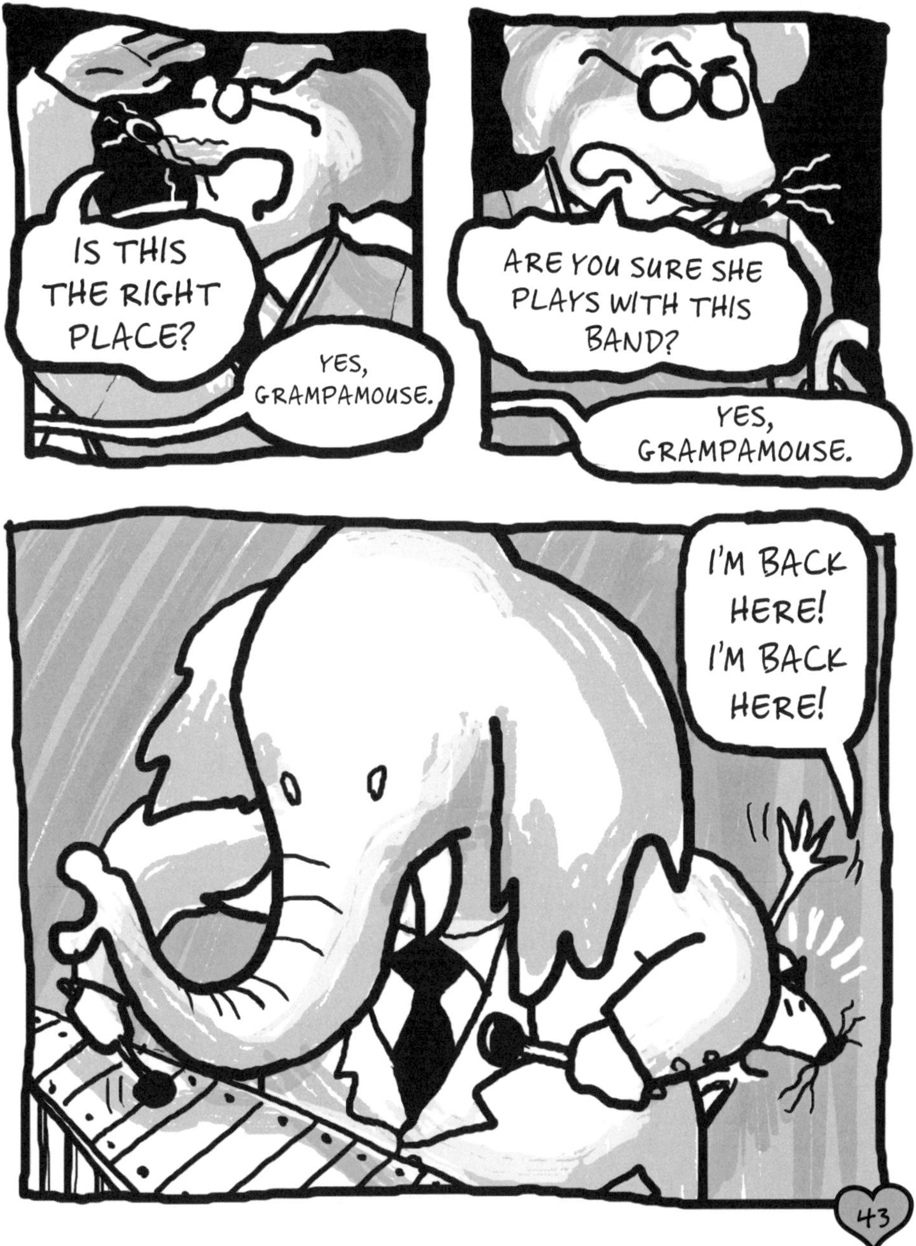
IS THIS THE RIGHT PLACE?
YES, GRAMPAMOUSE.
ARE YOU SURE SHE PLAYS WITH THIS BAND?
YES, GRAMPAMOUSE.
I'M BACK HERE! I'M BACK HERE!

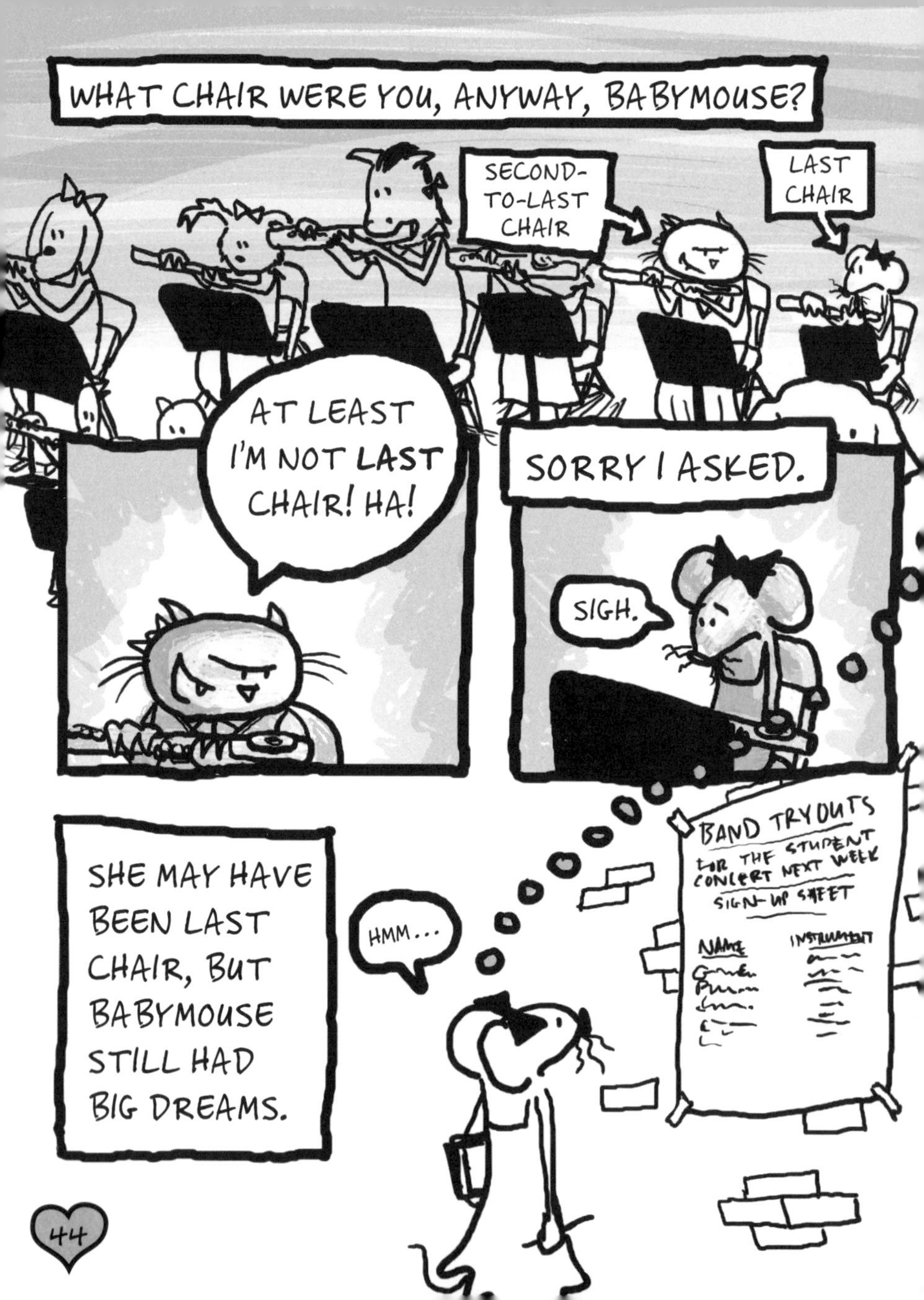
WHAT CHAIR WERE YOU, ANYWAY, BABYMOUSE?
SECOND-TO-LAST CHAIR
LAST CHAIR
AT LEAST I'M NOT **LAST** CHAIR! HA!
SORRY I ASKED.
SIGH.
SHE MAY HAVE BEEN LAST CHAIR, BUT BABYMOUSE STILL HAD BIG DREAMS.
HMM...
BAND TRYOUTS
FOR THE STUDENT CONCERT NEXT WEEK
SIGN-UP SHEET
NAME
INSTRUMENT

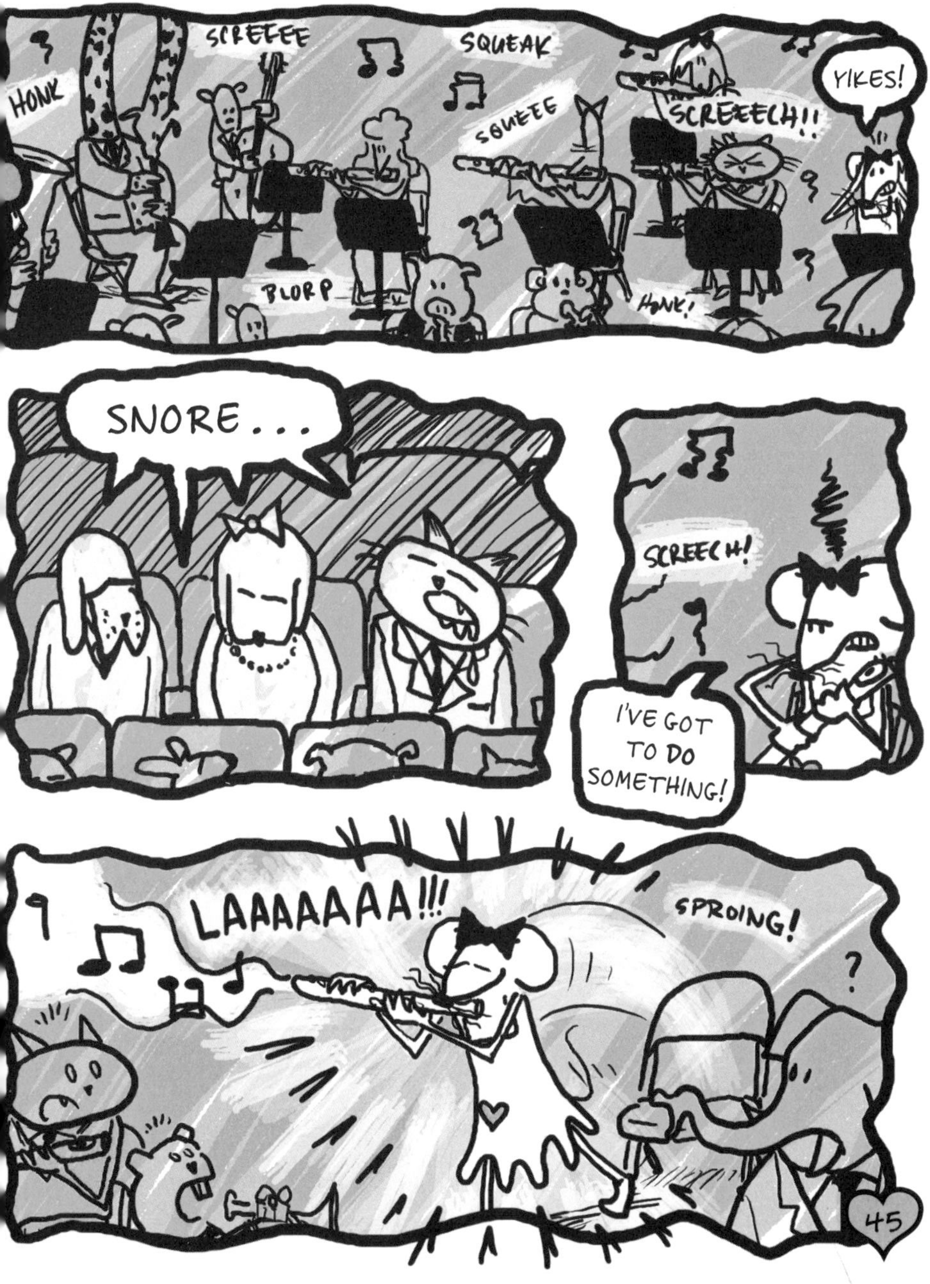
HONK
SCREEEE
SQUEAK
SQUEEE
SCREEECH!!
YIKES!
BLORP
HONK!
SNORE...
SCREECH!
I'VE GOT TO DO SOMETHING!
LAAAAAAA!!!
SPROING!
?

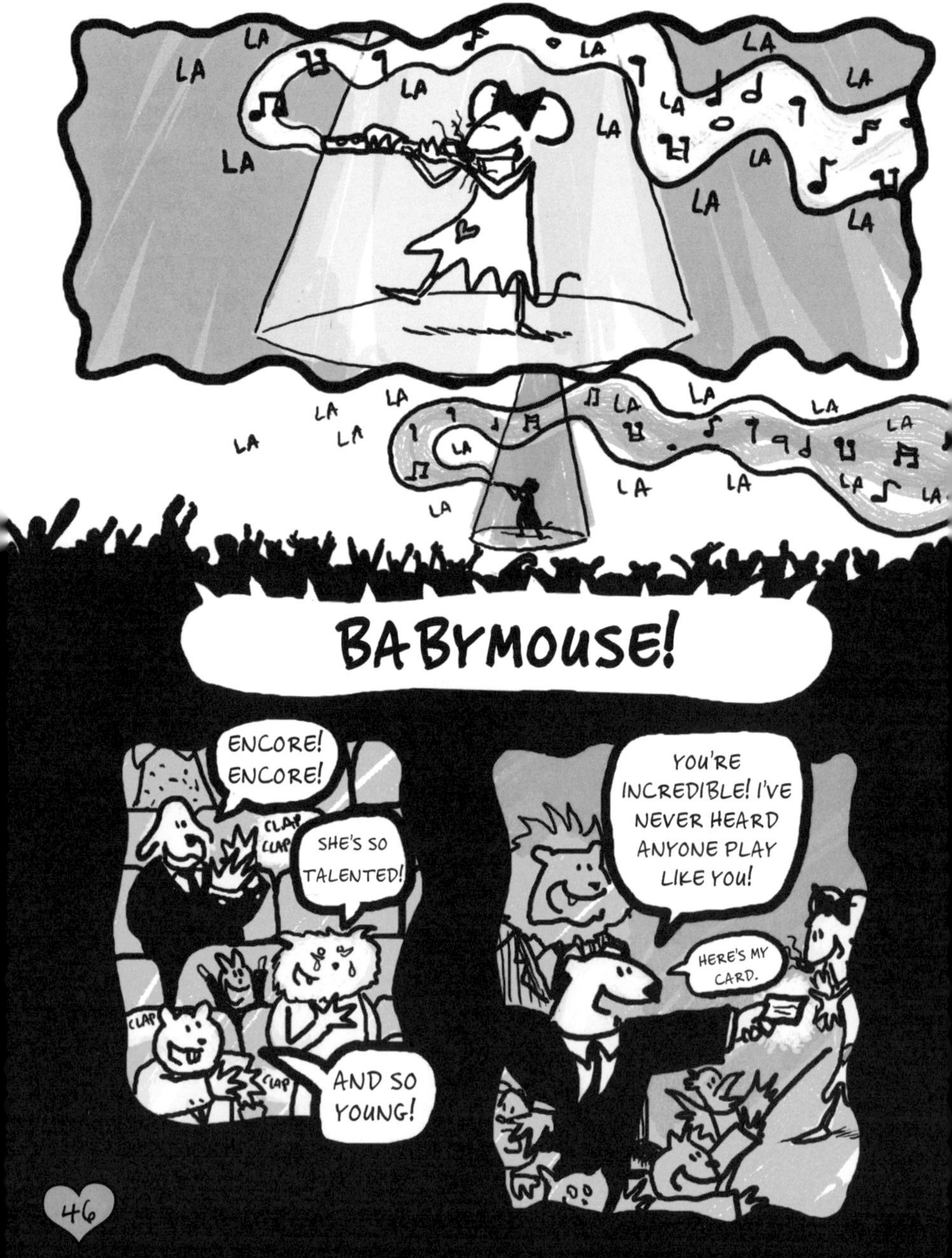
LA LA LA LA LA LA LA LA LA LA LA
LA LA LA LA LA LA LA LA LA LA LA LA LA LA LA
BABYMOUSE!
ENCORE! ENCORE!
CLAP CLAP
SHE'S SO TALENTED!
CLAP
CLAP
AND SO YOUNG!
YOU'RE INCREDIBLE! I'VE NEVER HEARD ANYONE PLAY LIKE YOU!
HERE'S MY CARD.

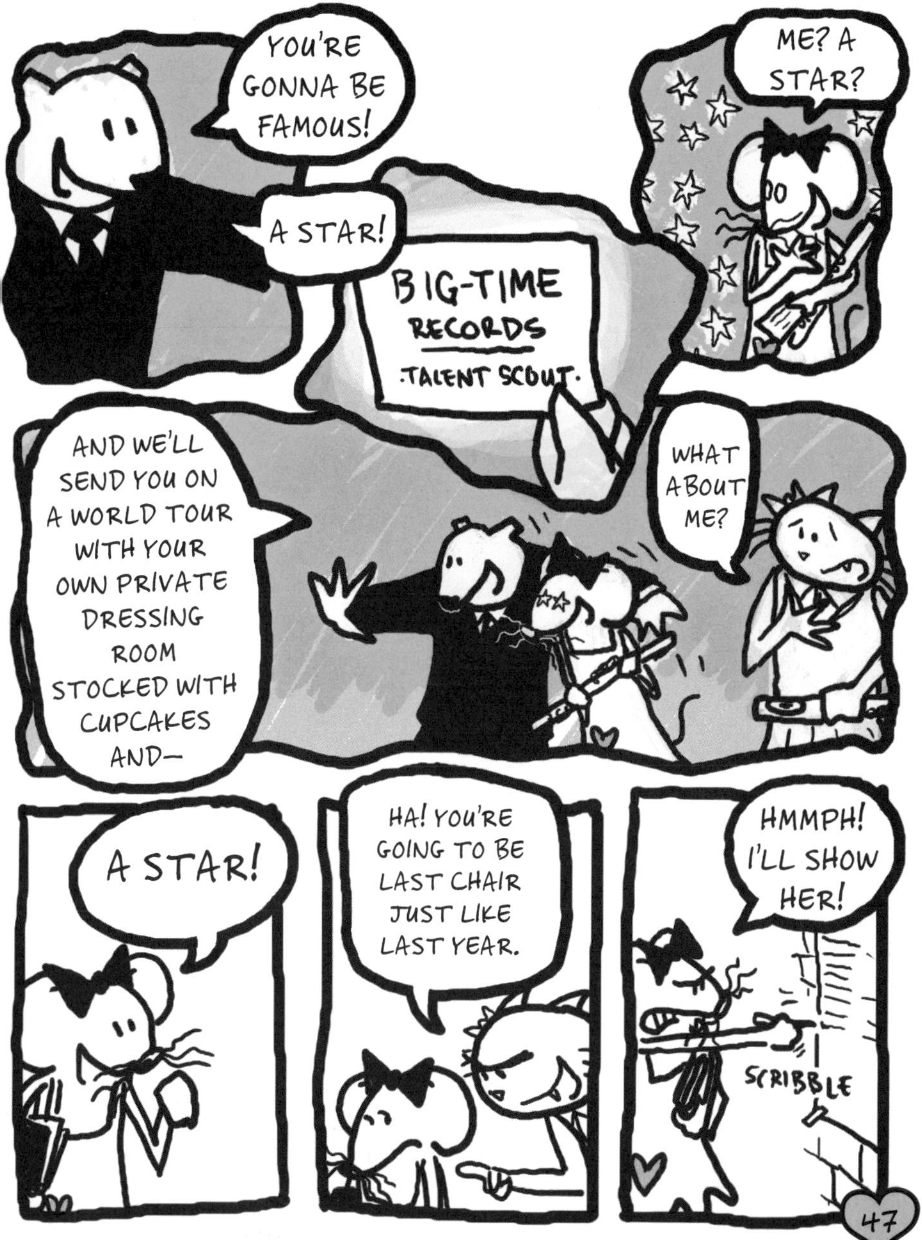

YOU'RE GONNA BE FAMOUS!
A STAR!
BIG-TIME RECORDS
·TALENT SCOUT·
ME? A STAR?
AND WE'LL SEND YOU ON A WORLD TOUR WITH YOUR OWN PRIVATE DRESSING ROOM STOCKED WITH CUPCAKES AND—
WHAT ABOUT ME?
A STAR!
HA! YOU'RE GOING TO BE LAST CHAIR JUST LIKE LAST YEAR.
HMMPH! I'LL SHOW HER!
SCRIBBLE

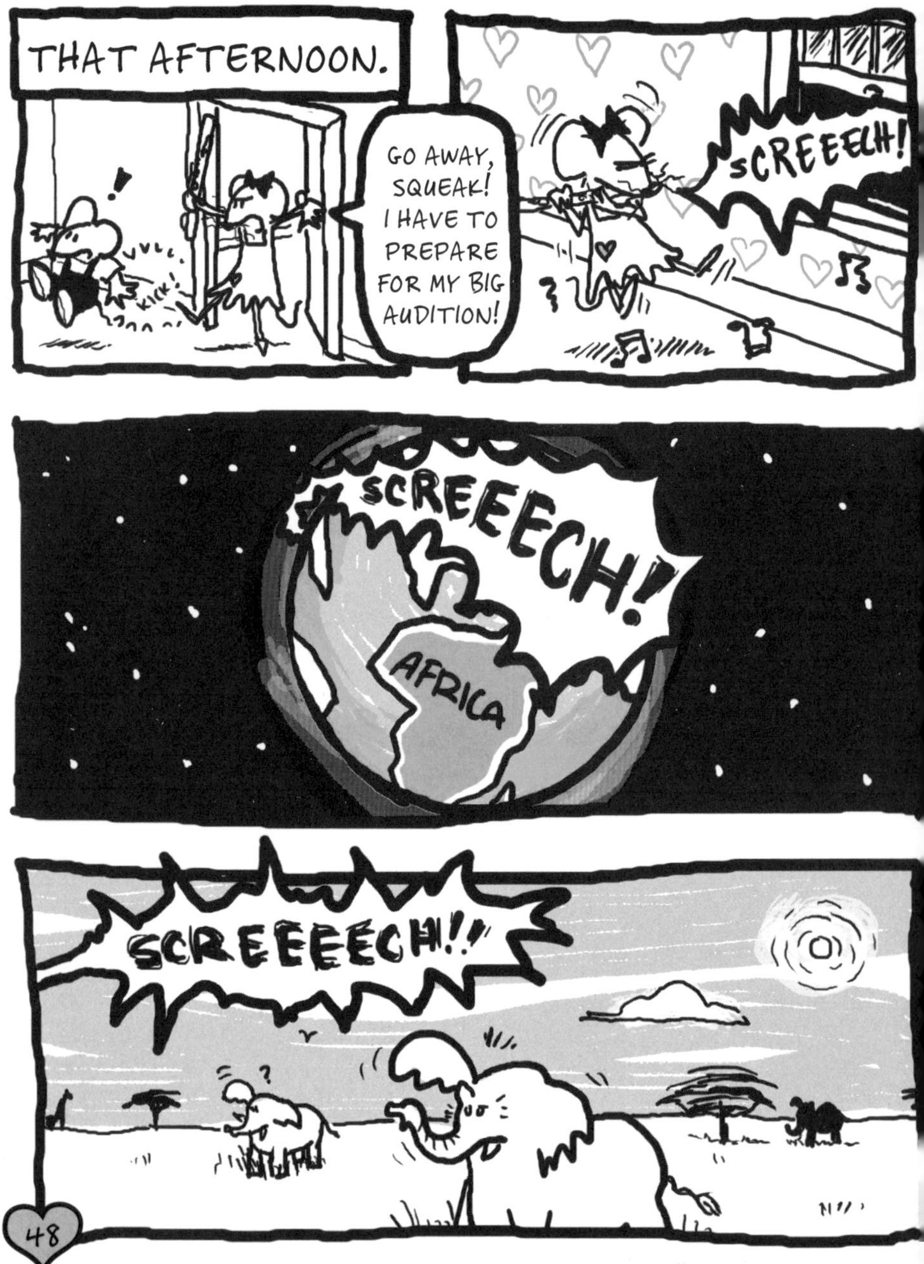
THAT AFTERNOON.
KICK
GO AWAY, SQUEAK! I HAVE TO PREPARE FOR MY BIG AUDITION!
SCREEECH!
SCREEECH!
AFRICA
SCREEEEECH!!

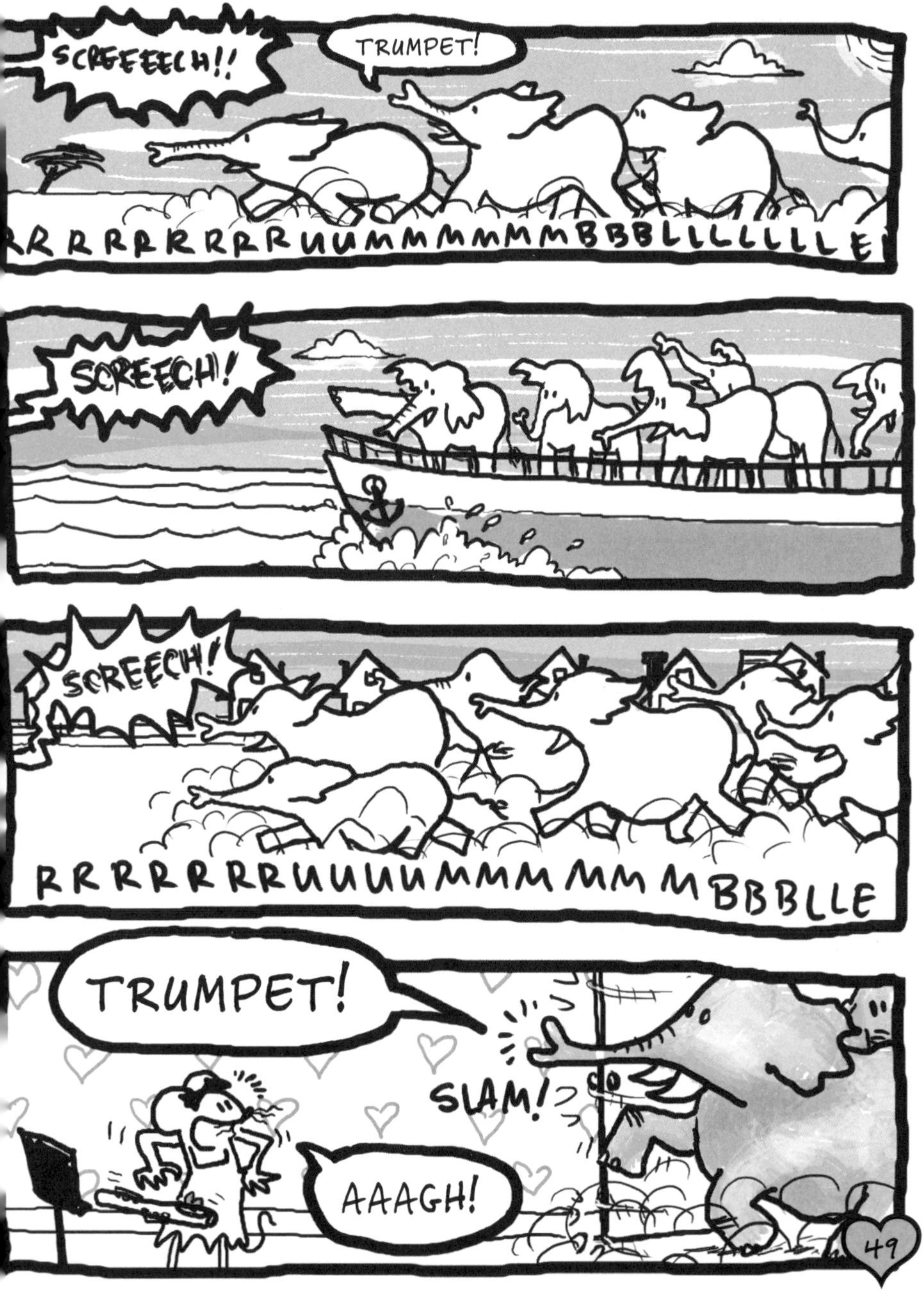
SCREEECH!!
TRUMPET!
RRRRRRRRUUMMMMMMBBBLLLLLLLE
SCREECH!
SCREECH!
RRRRRRRUUUUUMMMMMMMBBBLLE
TRUMPET!
SLAM!
AAAGH!

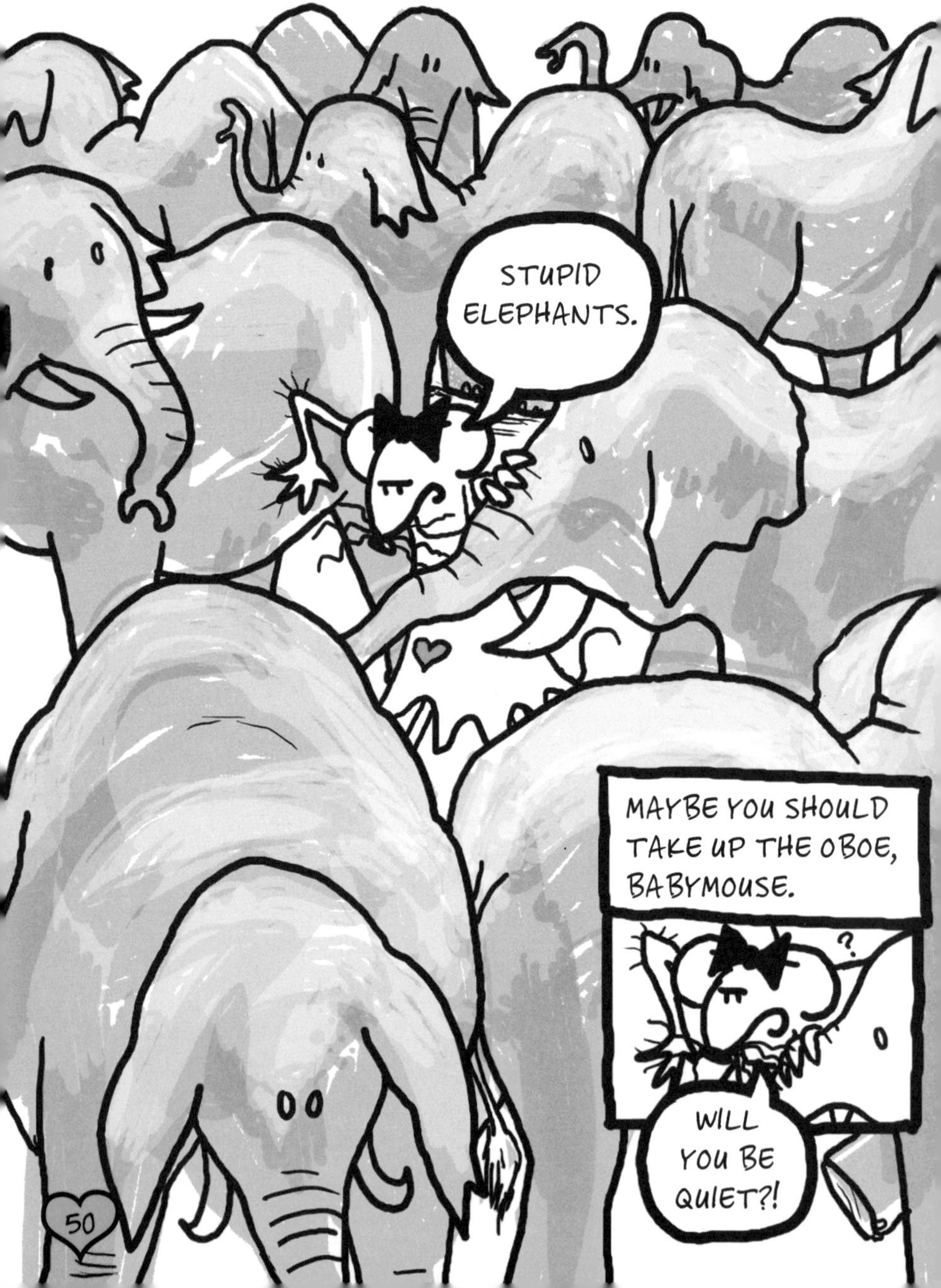
STUPID ELEPHANTS.
MAYBE YOU SHOULD TAKE UP THE OBOE, BABYMOUSE.
?
WILL YOU BE QUIET?!

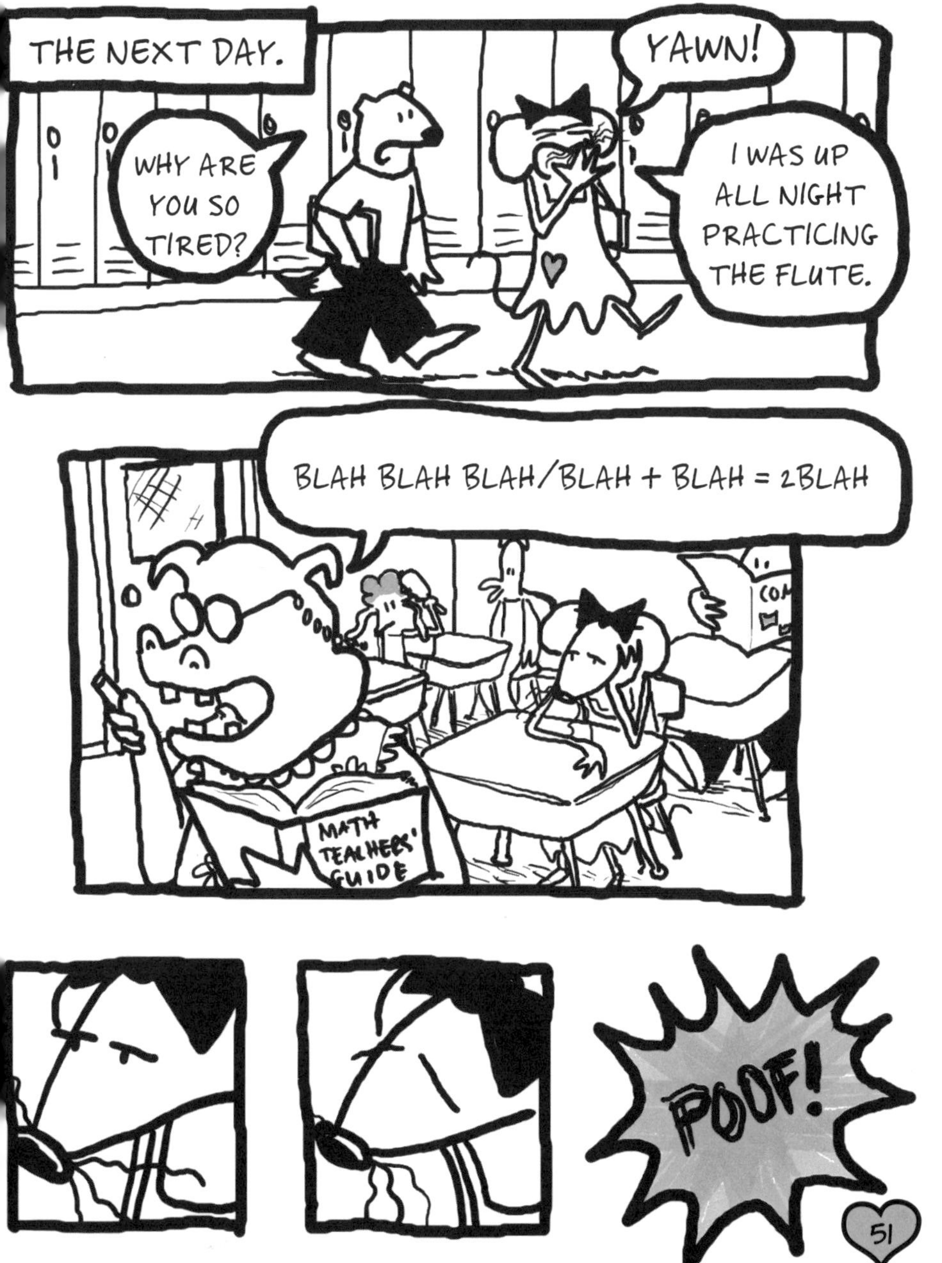

THE NEXT DAY.
YAWN!
WHY ARE YOU SO TIRED?
I WAS UP ALL NIGHT PRACTICING THE FLUTE.
BLAH BLAH BLAH/BLAH + BLAH = 2BLAH
MATH TEACHERS' GUIDE
POOF!

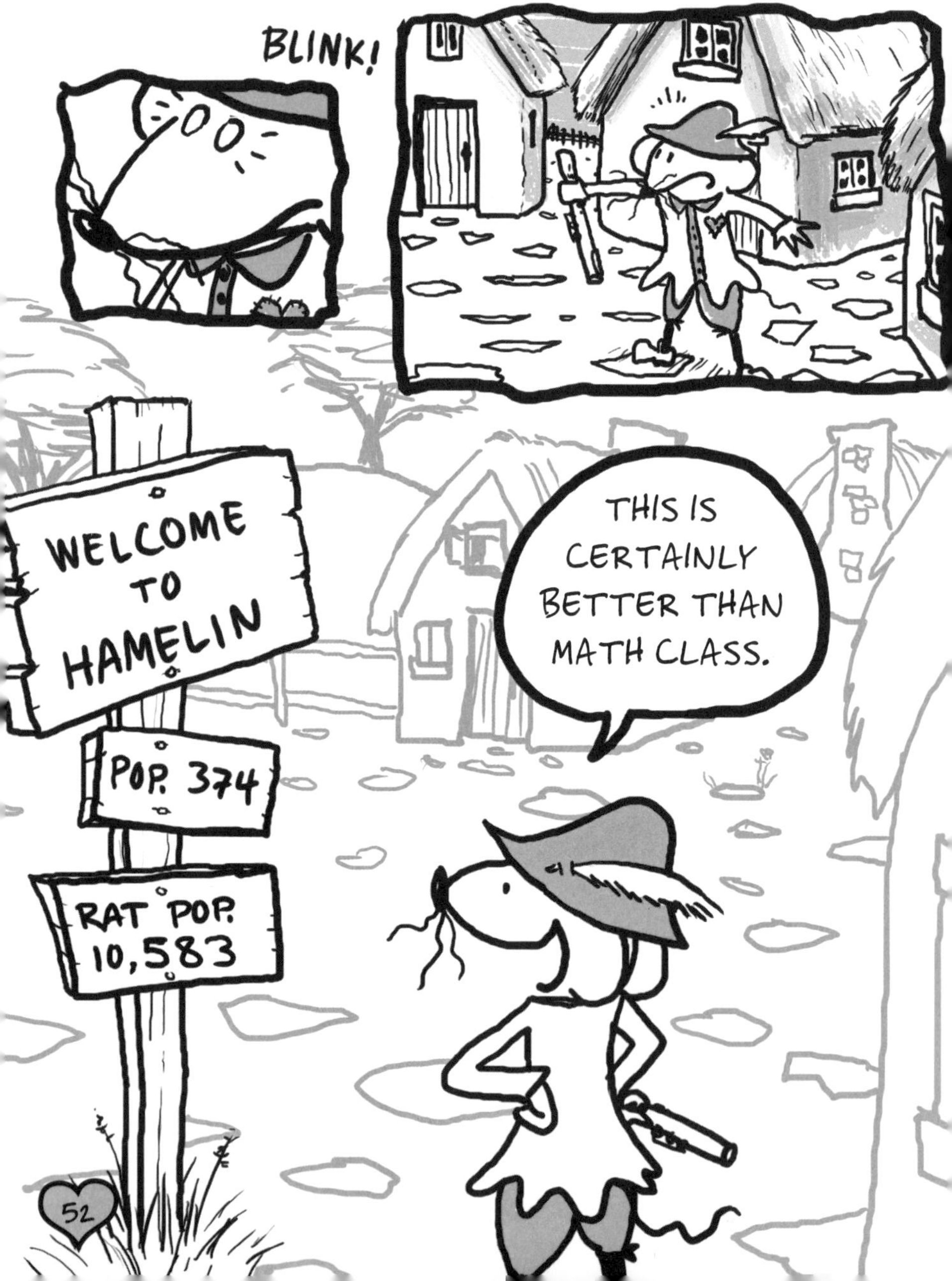
BLINK!
WELCOME TO HAMELIN
POP. 374
RAT POP. 10,583
THIS IS CERTAINLY BETTER THAN MATH CLASS.

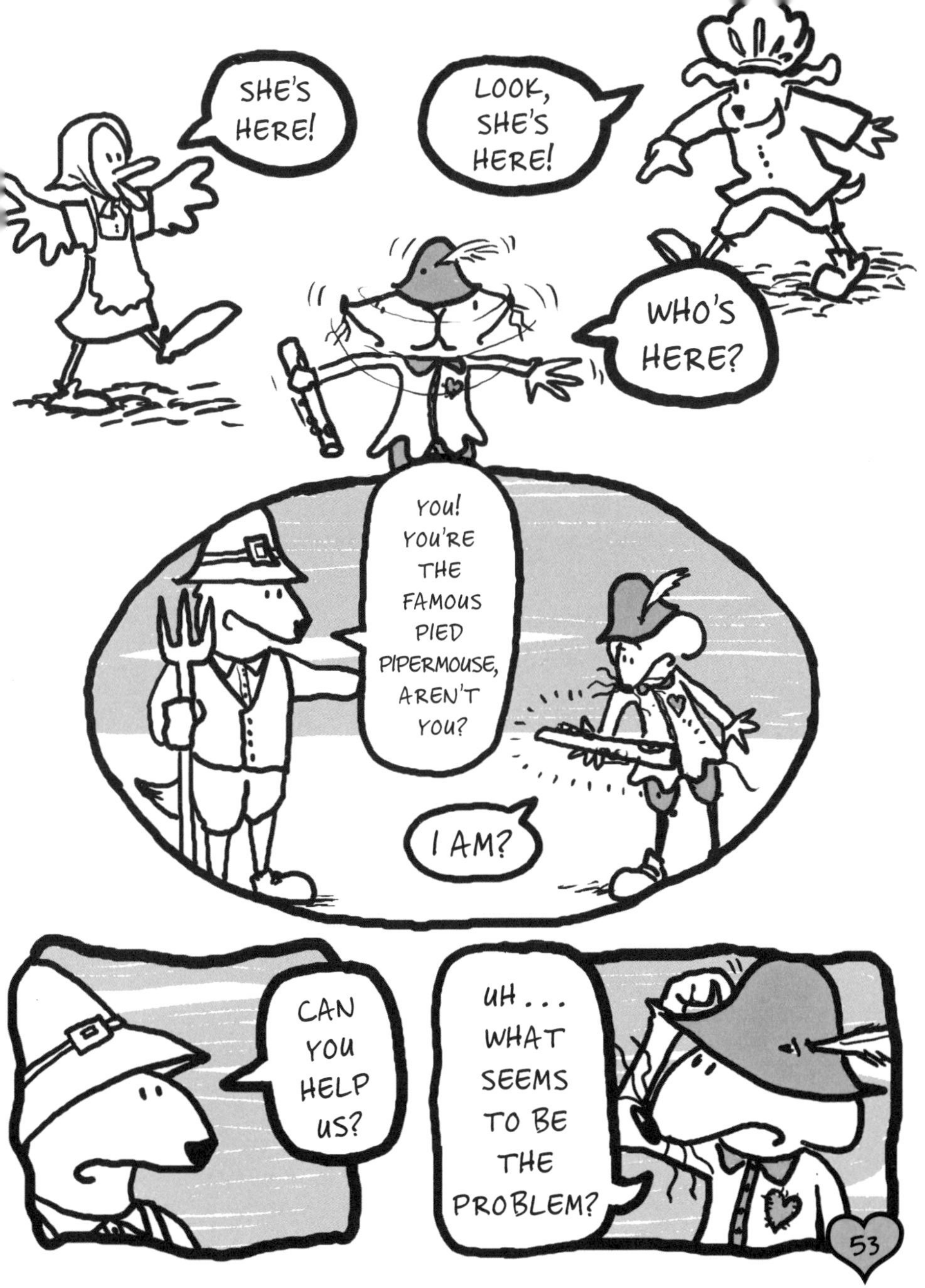
SHE'S HERE!
LOOK, SHE'S HERE!
WHO'S HERE?
YOU! YOU'RE THE FAMOUS PIED PIPERMOUSE, AREN'T YOU?
I AM?
CAN YOU HELP US?
UH . . . WHAT SEEMS TO BE THE PROBLEM?

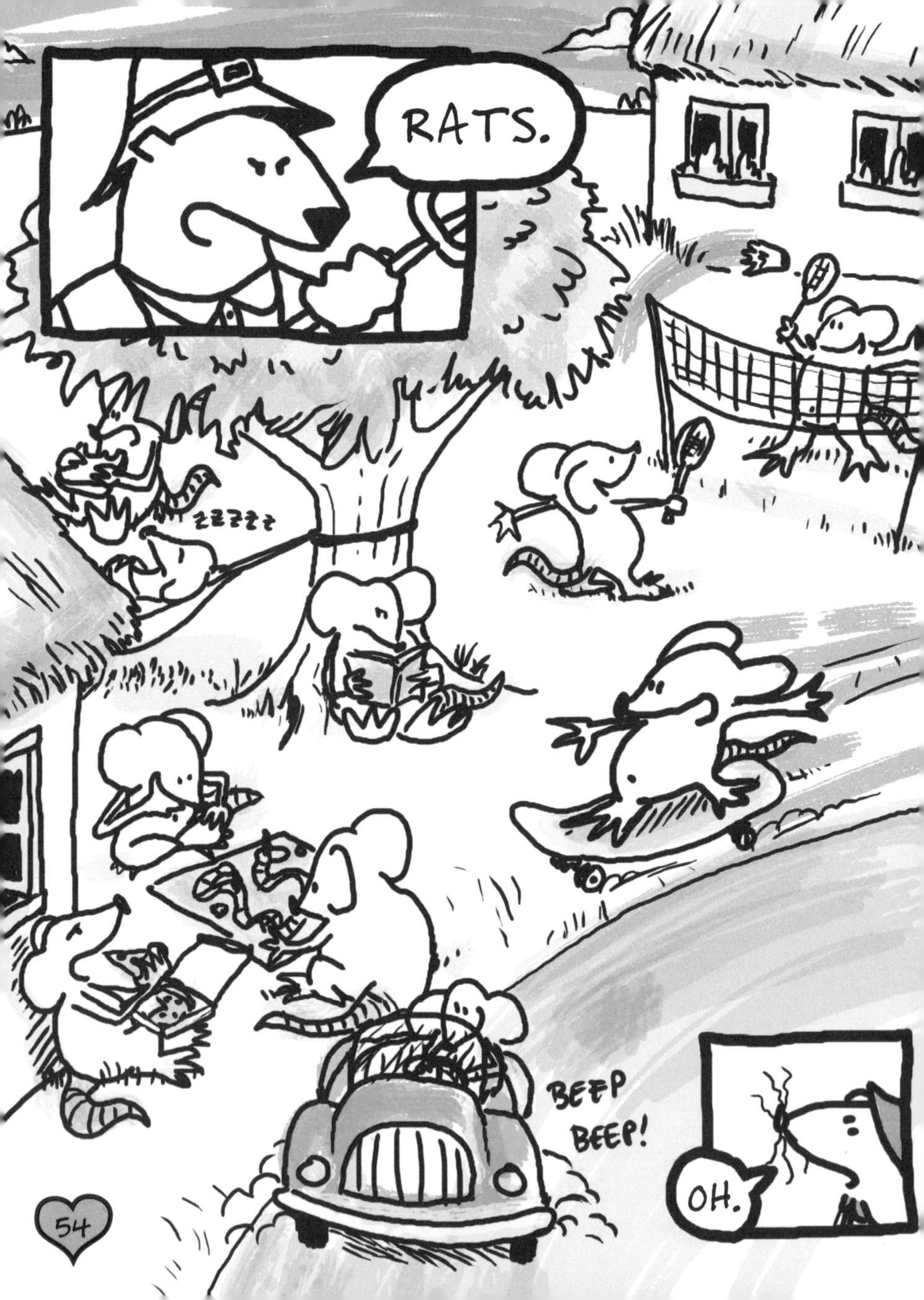
RATS.
ZZZZZZ
BEEP
BEEP!
OH.

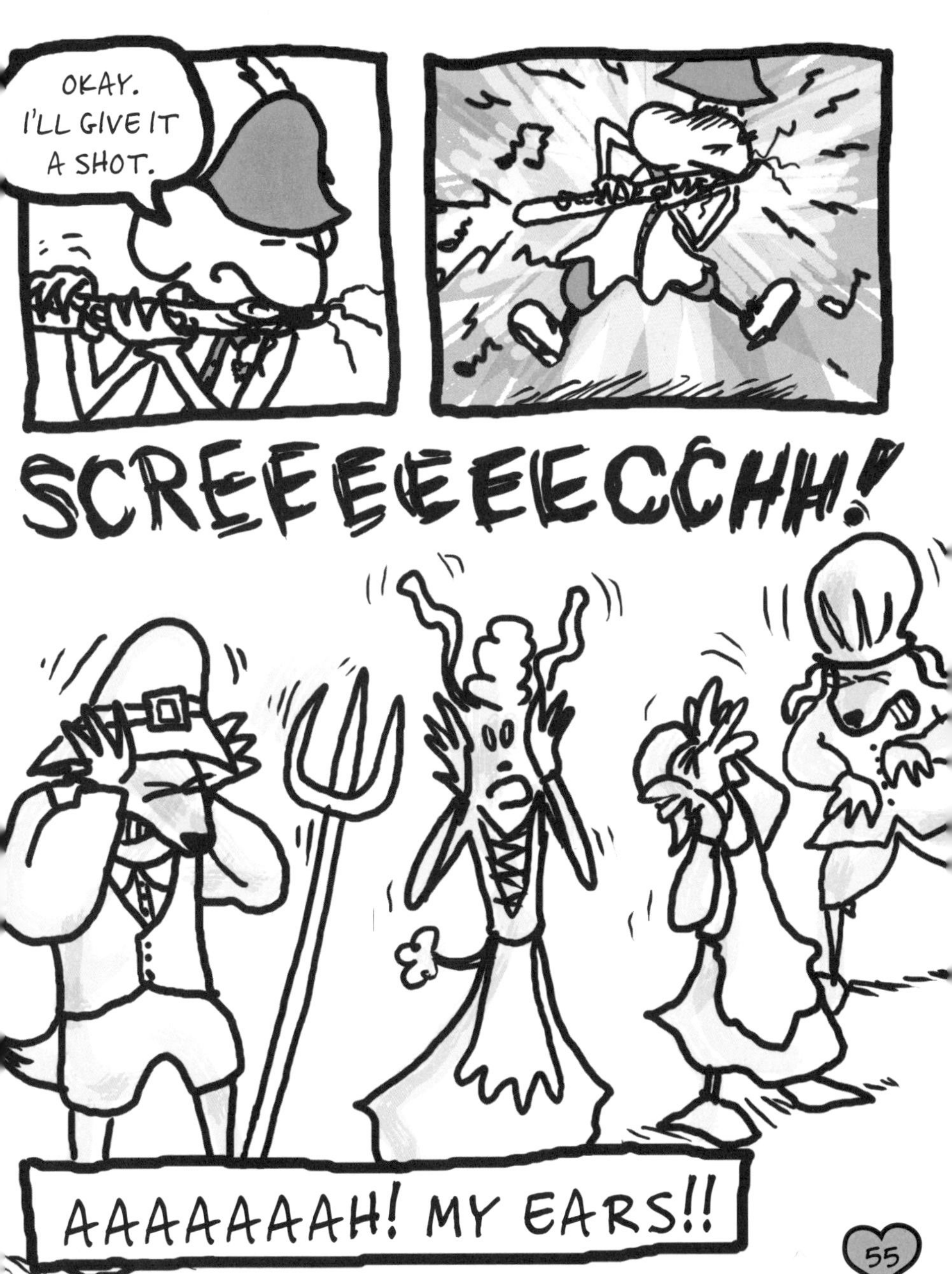
OKAY. I'LL GIVE IT A SHOT.
SCREEEEEEECCHH!
AAAAAAAH! MY EARS!!

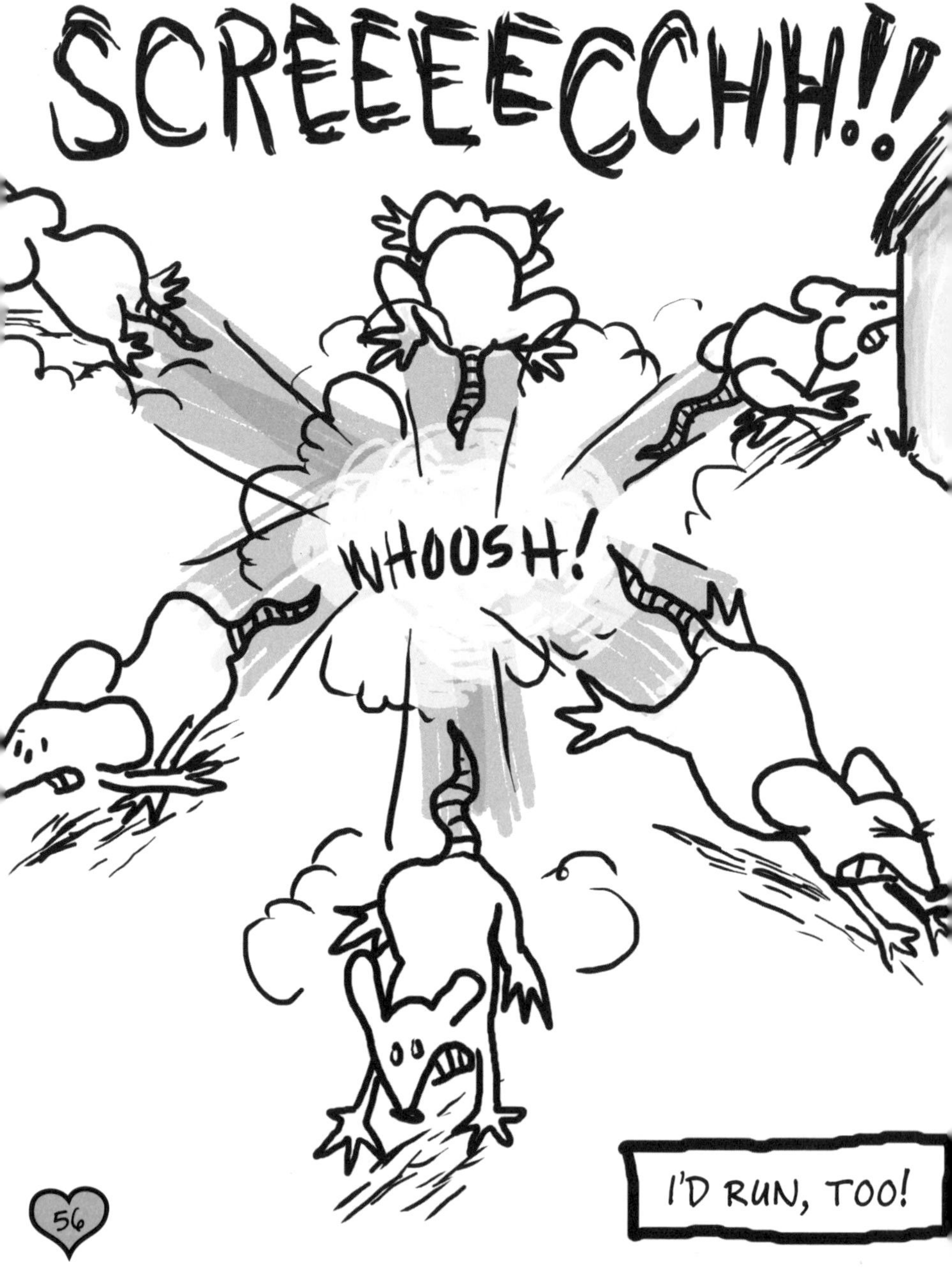
SCREEEECCHH!!
WHOOSH!
I'D RUN, TOO!

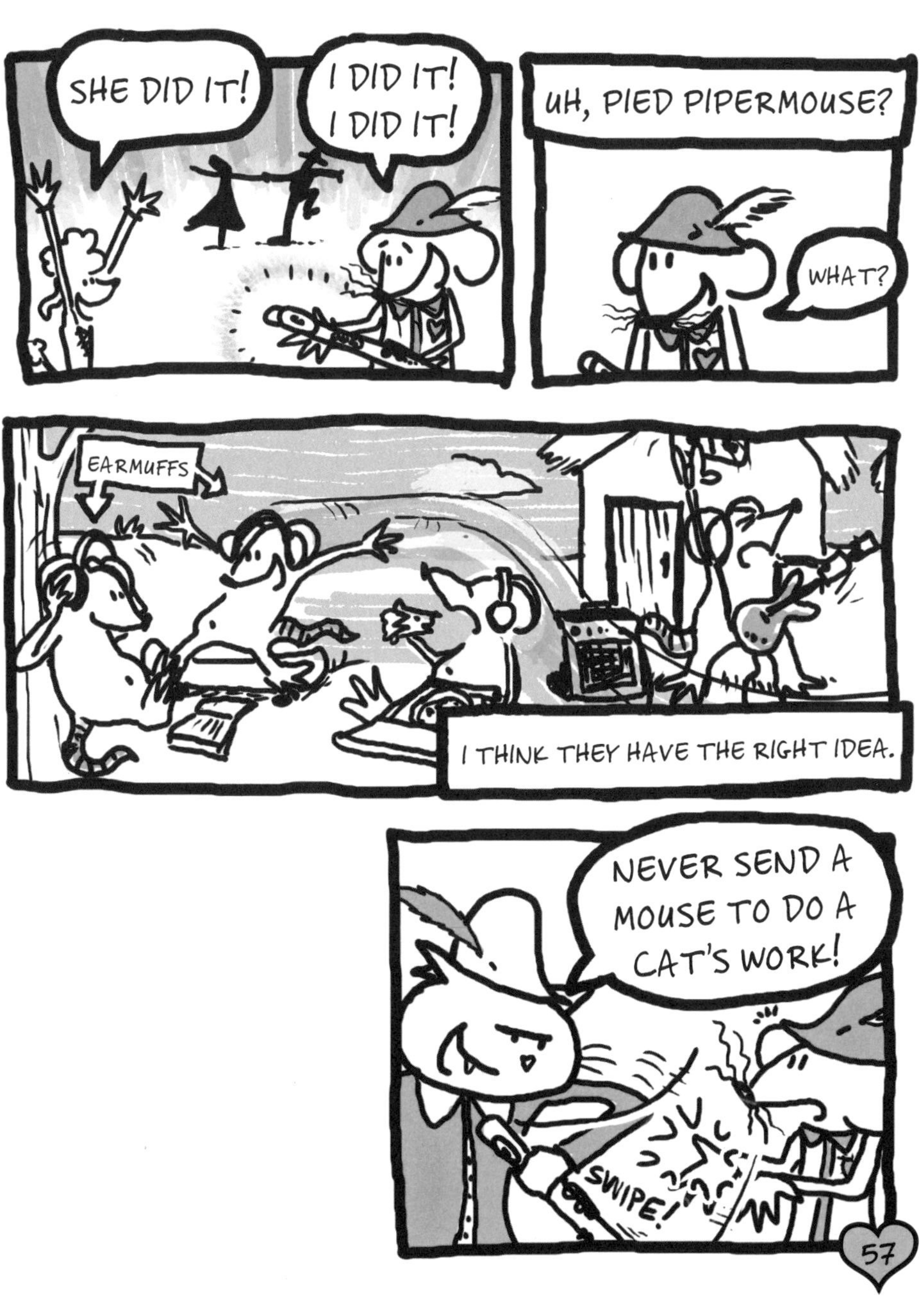

SHE DID IT!
I DID IT! I DID IT!
UH, PIED PIPERMOUSE?
WHAT?
EARMUFFS
I THINK THEY HAVE THE RIGHT IDEA.
NEVER SEND A MOUSE TO DO A CAT'S WORK!
SWIPE!

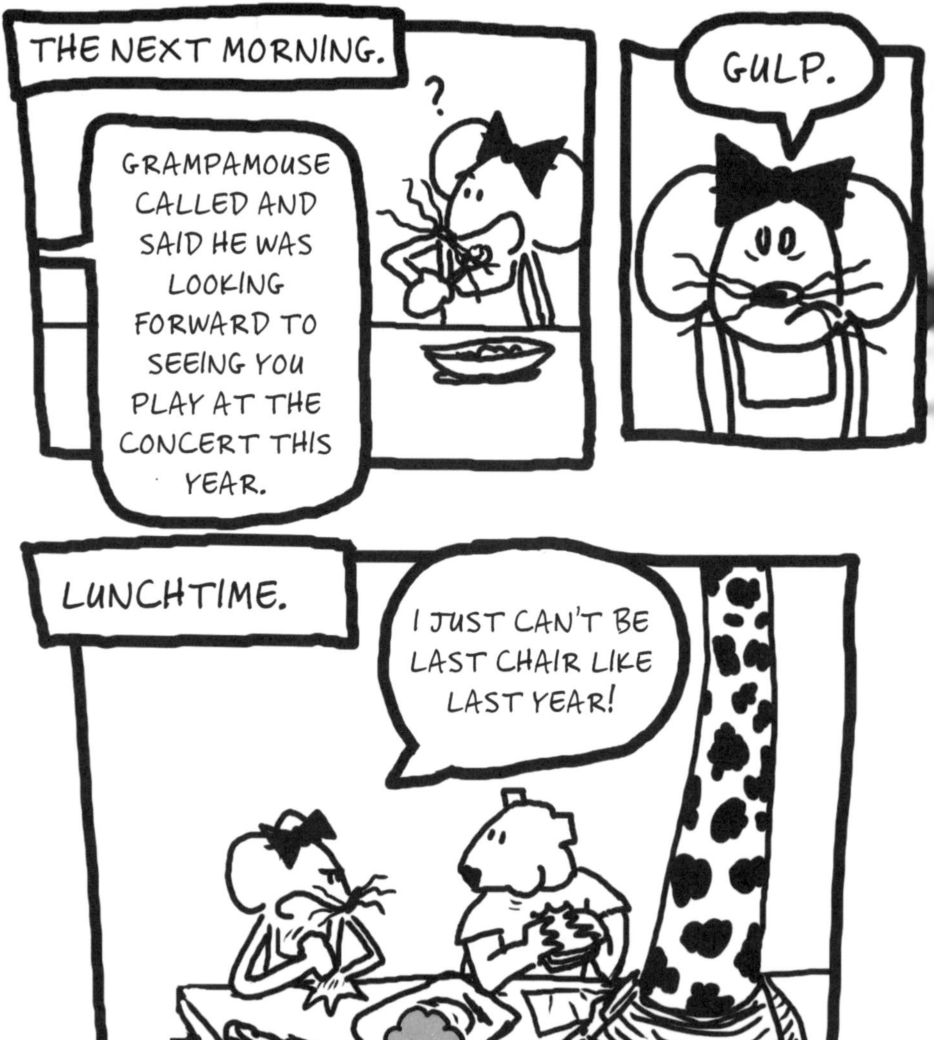
THE NEXT MORNING.
?
GRAMPAMOUSE CALLED AND SAID HE WAS LOOKING FORWARD TO SEEING YOU PLAY AT THE CONCERT THIS YEAR.
GULP.
LUNCHTIME.
I JUST CAN'T BE LAST CHAIR LIKE LAST YEAR!

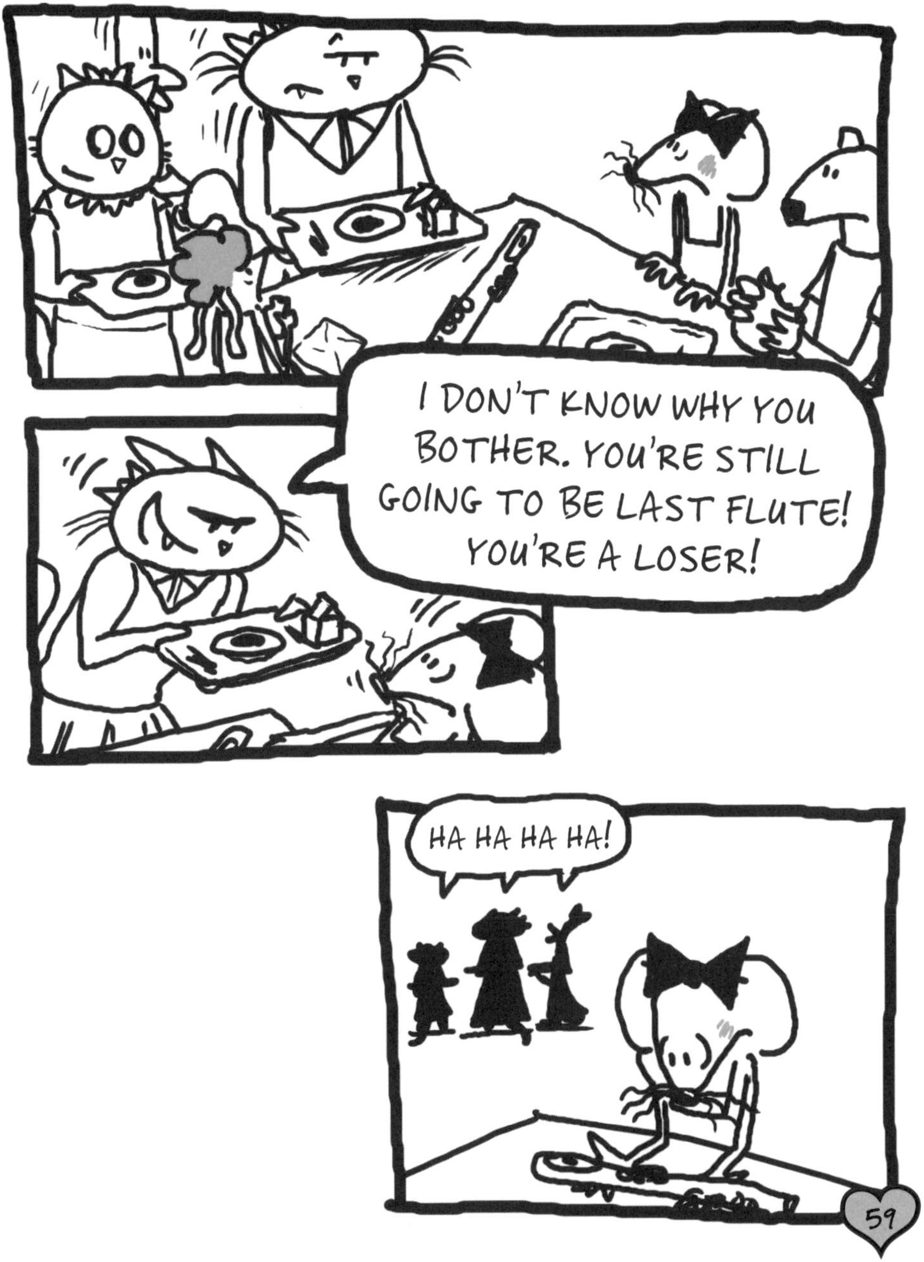
I DON'T KNOW WHY YOU BOTHER. YOU'RE STILL GOING TO BE LAST FLUTE! YOU'RE A LOSER!
HA HA HA HA!

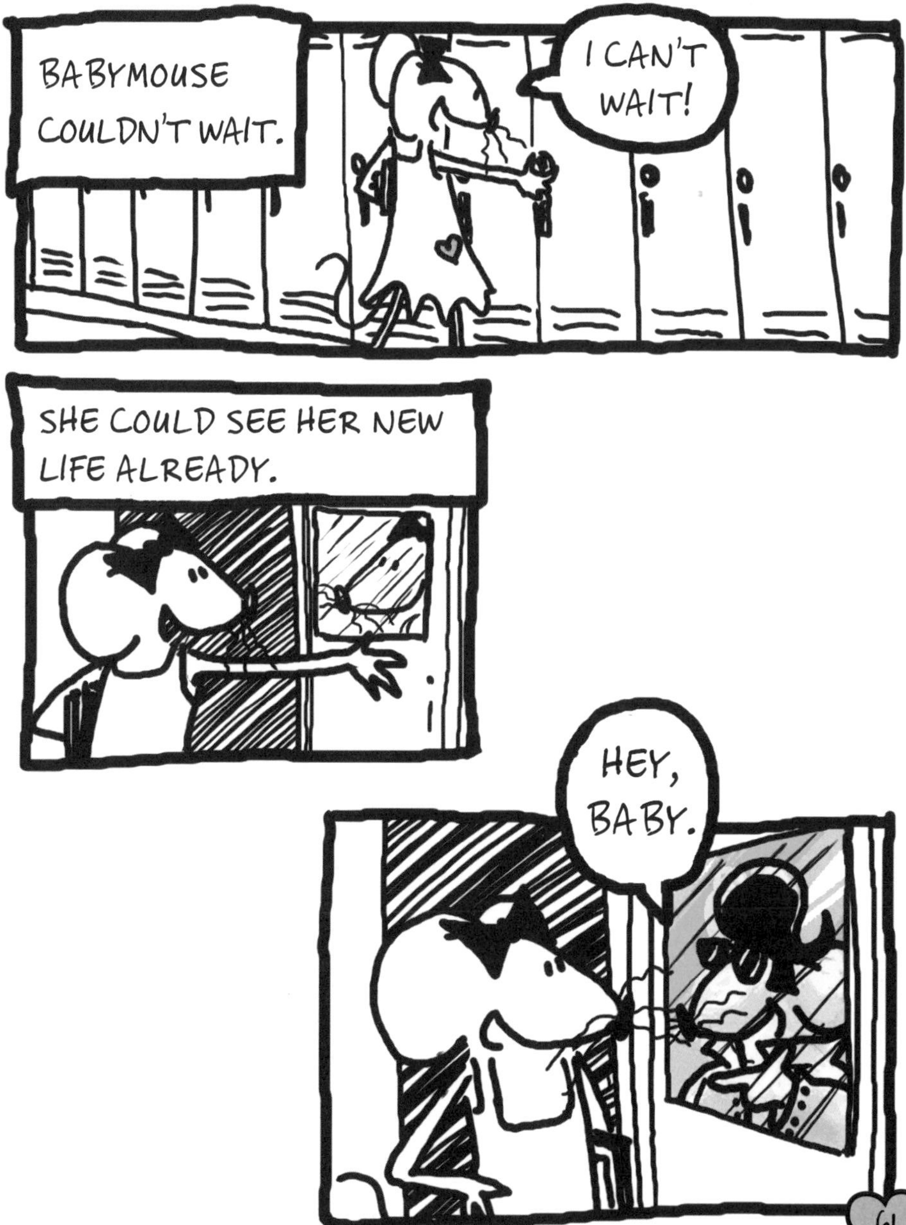
BABYMOUSE COULDN'T WAIT.
I CAN'T WAIT!
SHE COULD SEE HER NEW LIFE ALREADY.
HEY, BABY.

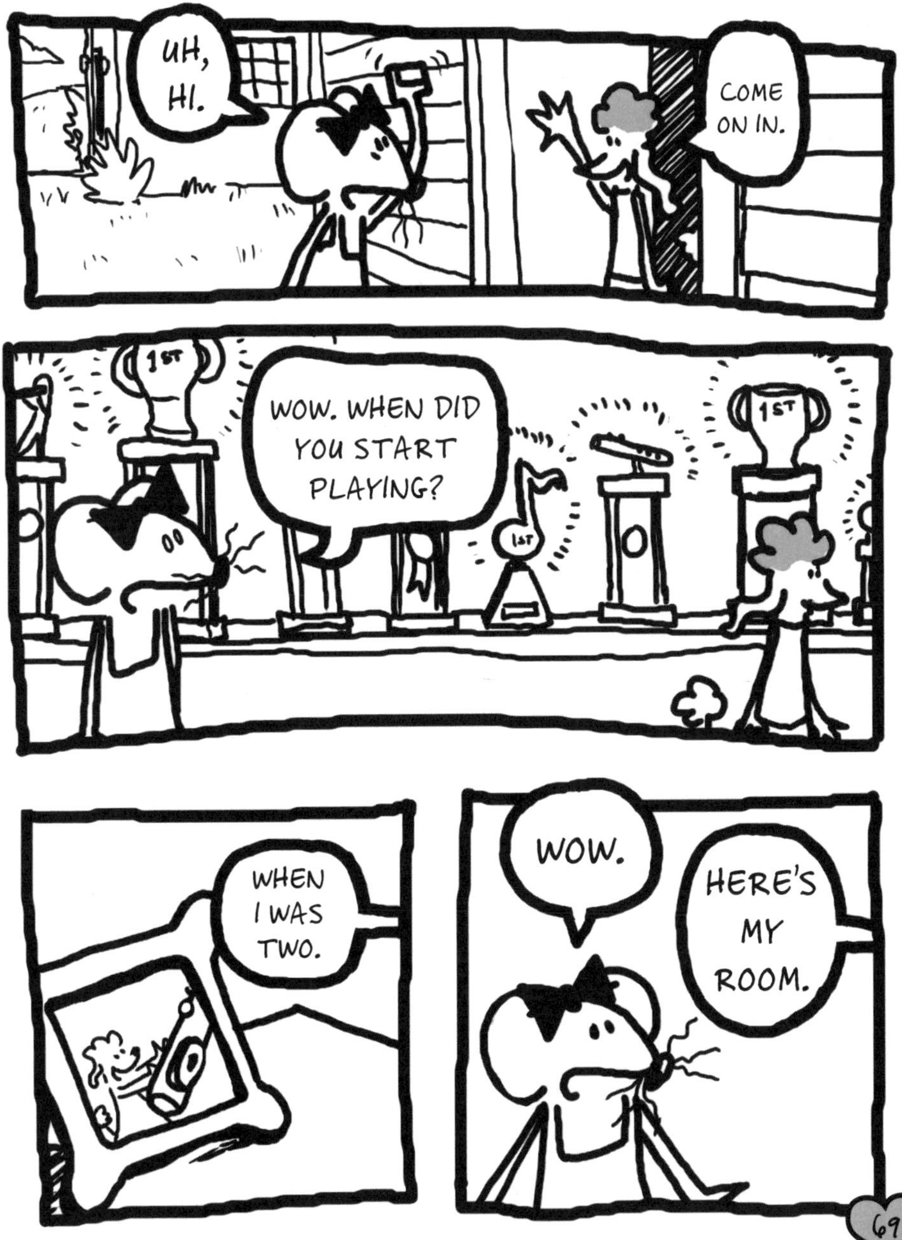
UH, HI.
COME ON IN.
WOW. WHEN DID YOU START PLAYING?
1ST
1ST
1ST
WHEN I WAS TWO.
WOW.
HERE'S MY ROOM.

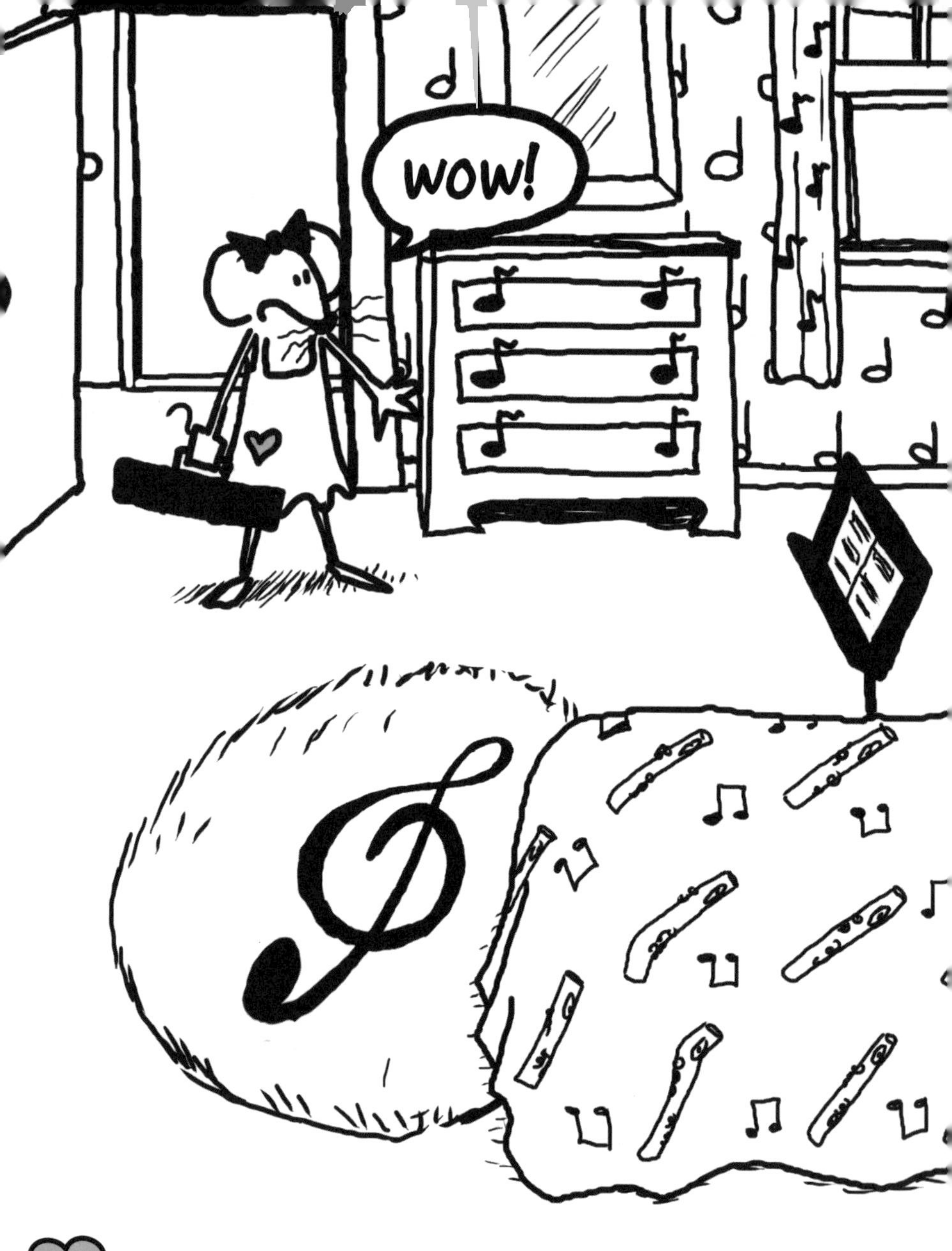
WOW!

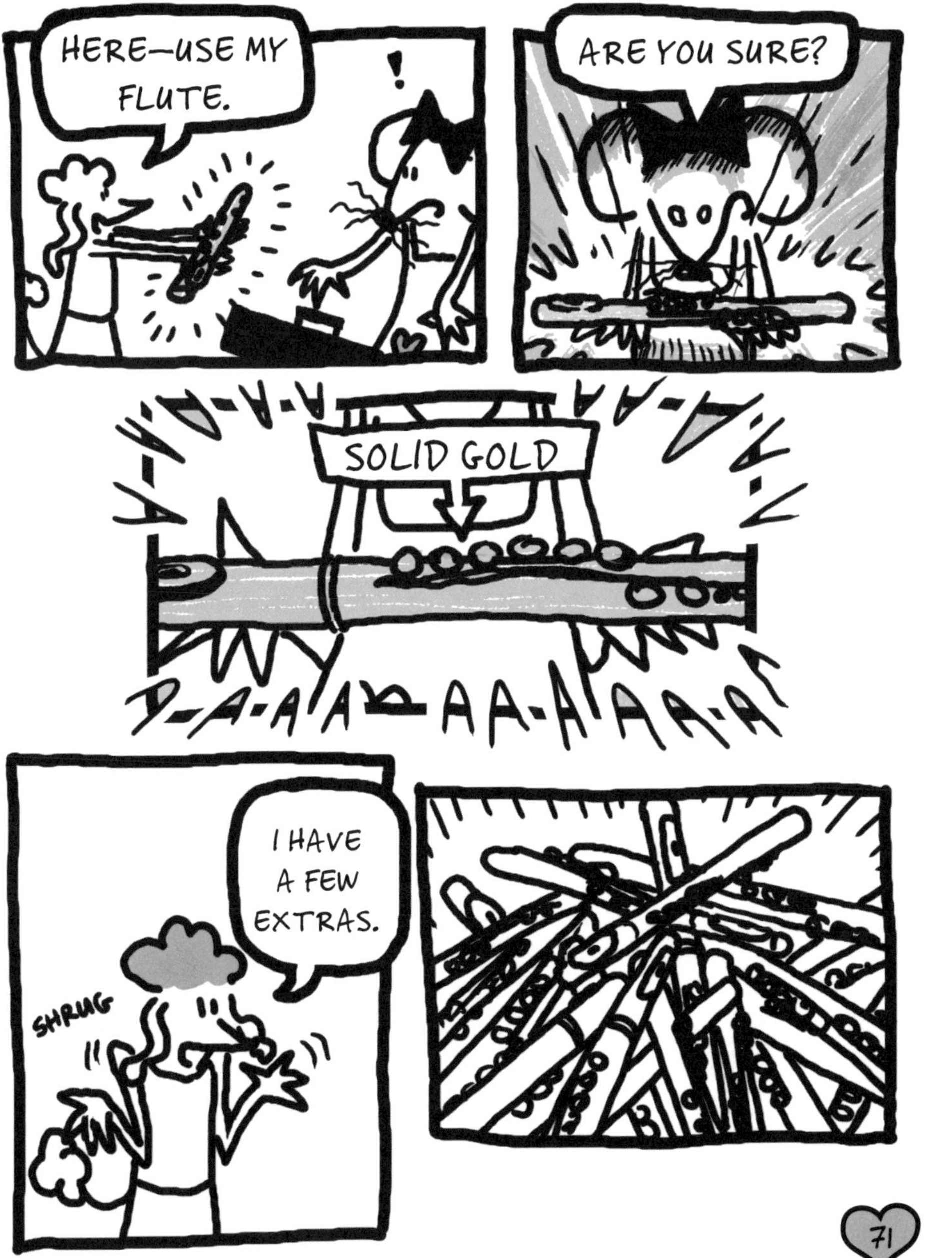
HERE—USE MY FLUTE.
!
ARE YOU SURE?
SOLID GOLD
I HAVE A FEW EXTRAS.
SHRUG

LET ME HEAR YOU PLAY, BABYMOUSE.

LET ME GET MY EARPLUGS, BABYMOUSE.

SCREEECH!!

AAAAAGGHH!

I THINK I KNOW WHAT'S WRONG.

NOD NOD

WELL, I CERTAINLY HOPE SO. I DON'T THINK I CAN STAND MUCH MORE OF THIS.

HEY!

72

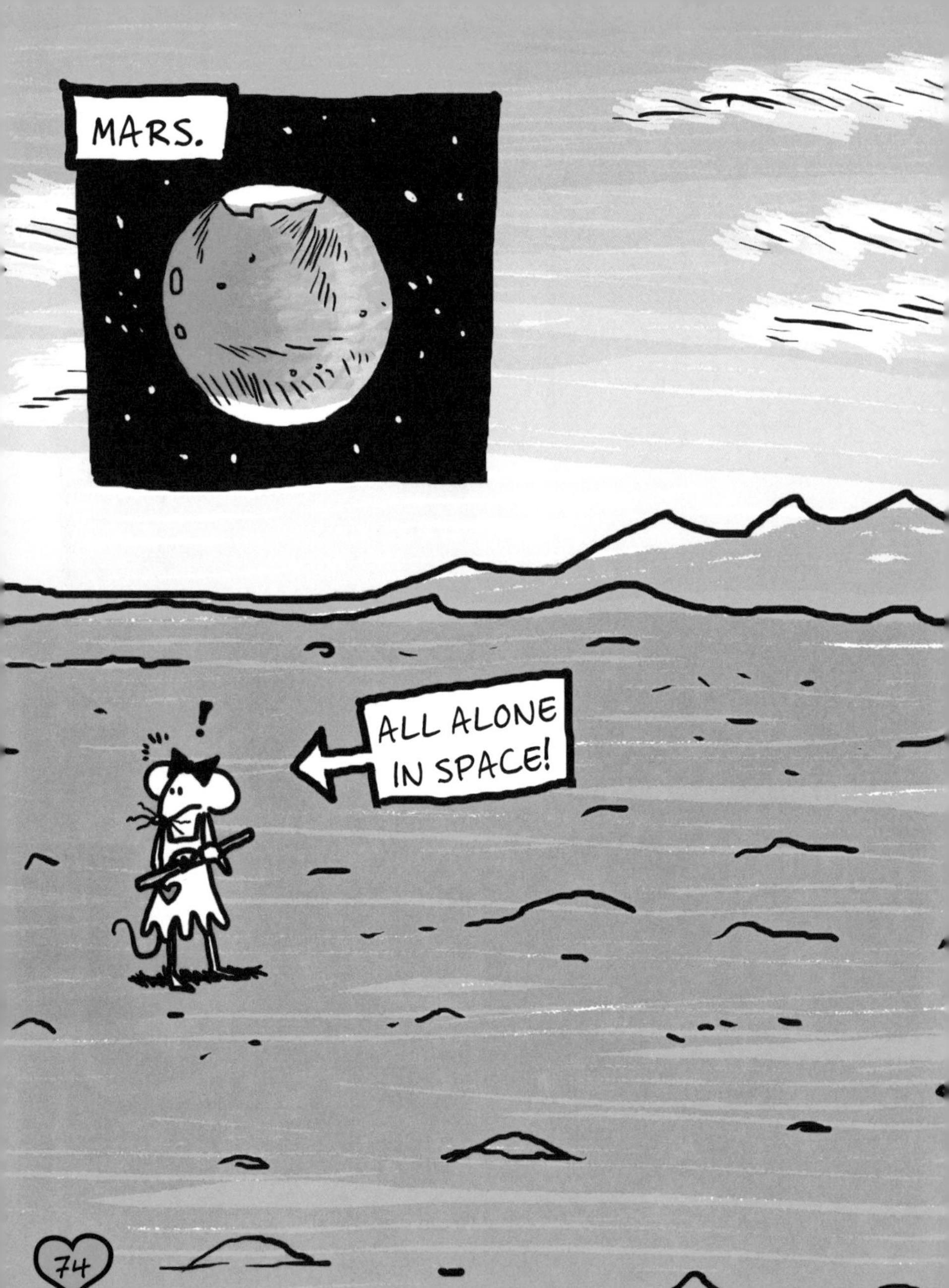
MARS.
!
ALL ALONE IN SPACE!

75

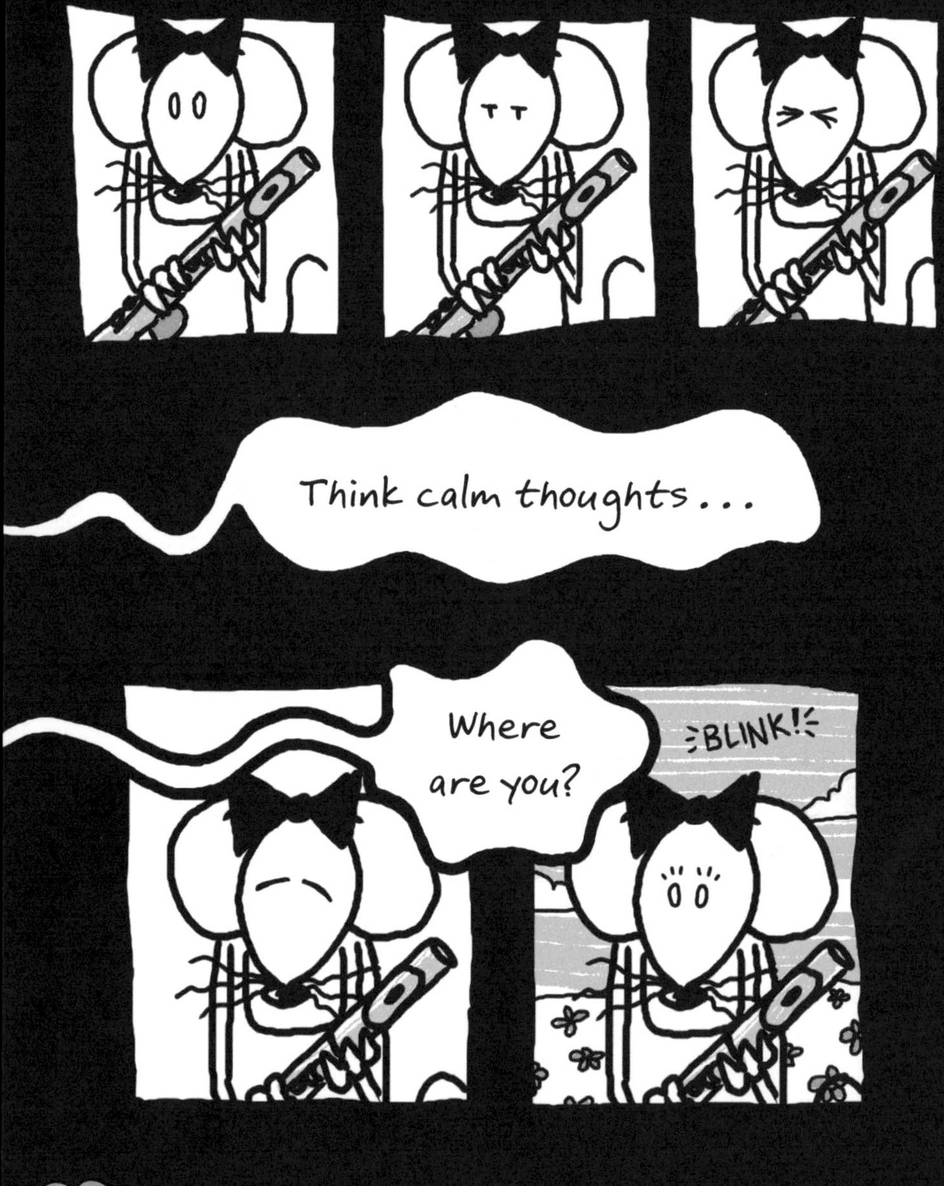
Think calm thoughts...
Where are you?
BLINK!

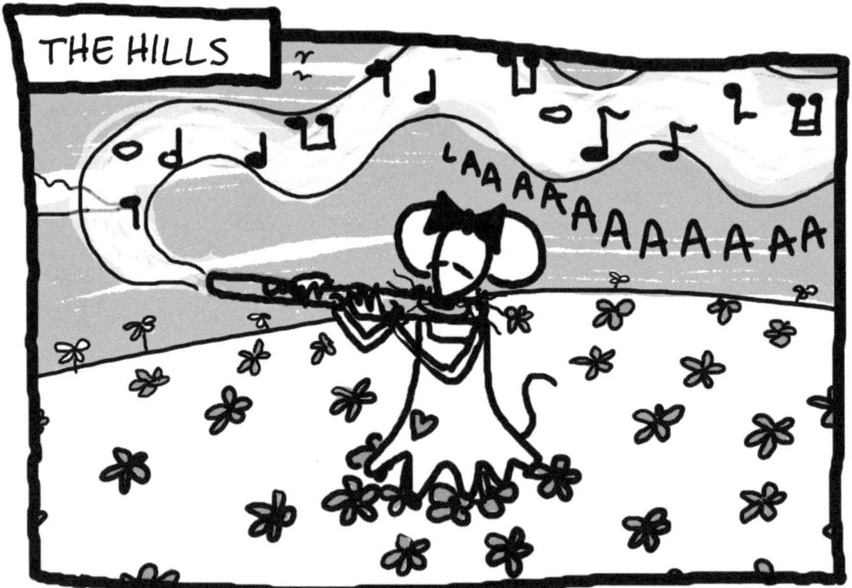
THE HILLS
LAAAAAAAAAAAAA

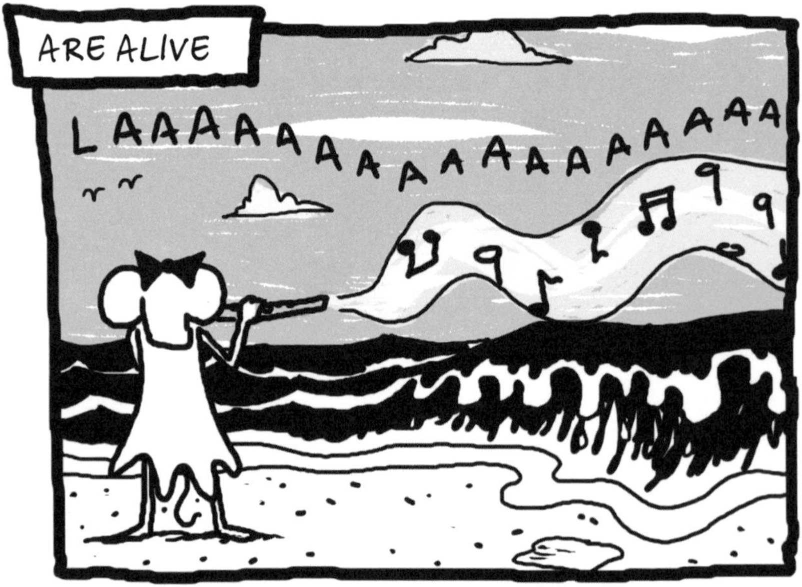
ARE ALIVE
LAAAAAAAAAAAAAAAAAAA

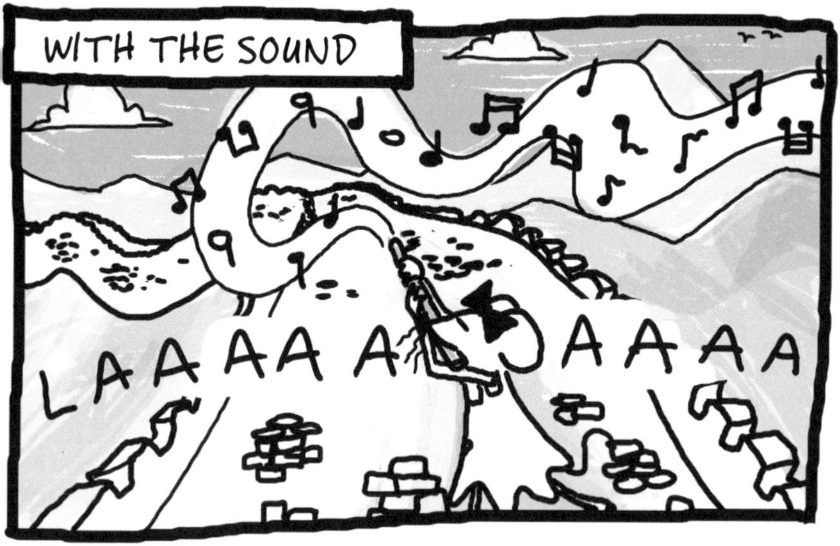
WITH THE SOUND
LAAAAAAAAAA

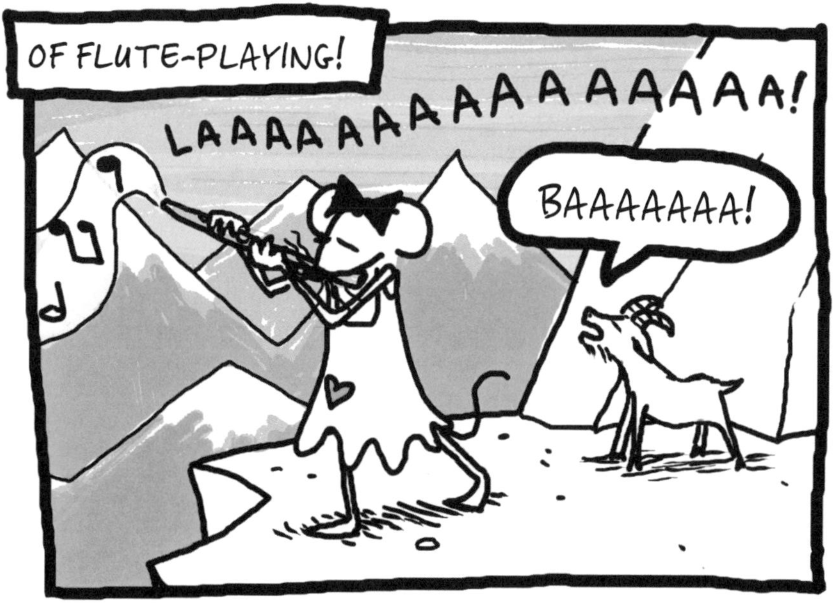
OF FLUTE-PLAYING!
LAAAAAAAAAAAAAA!
BAAAAAAA!

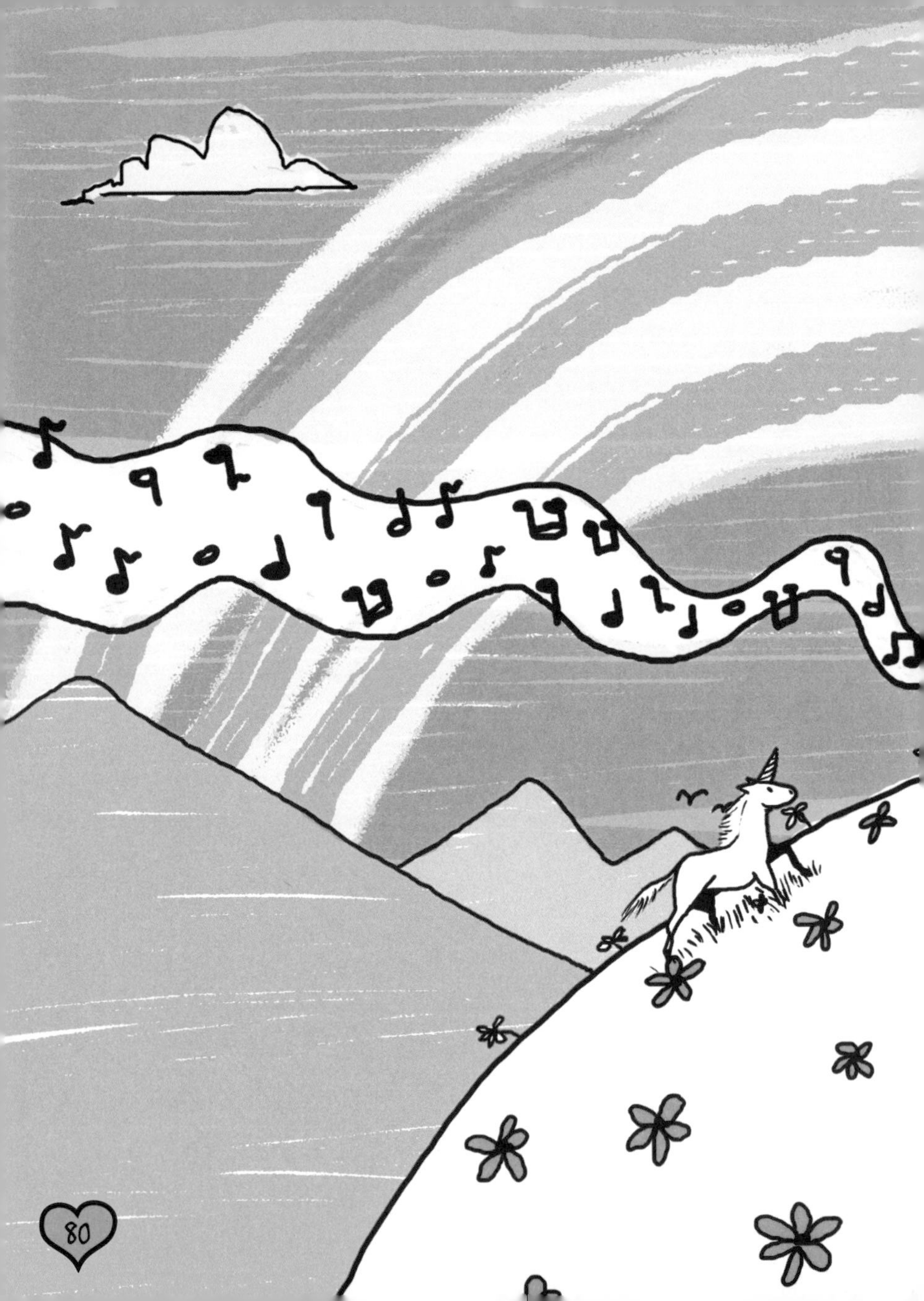

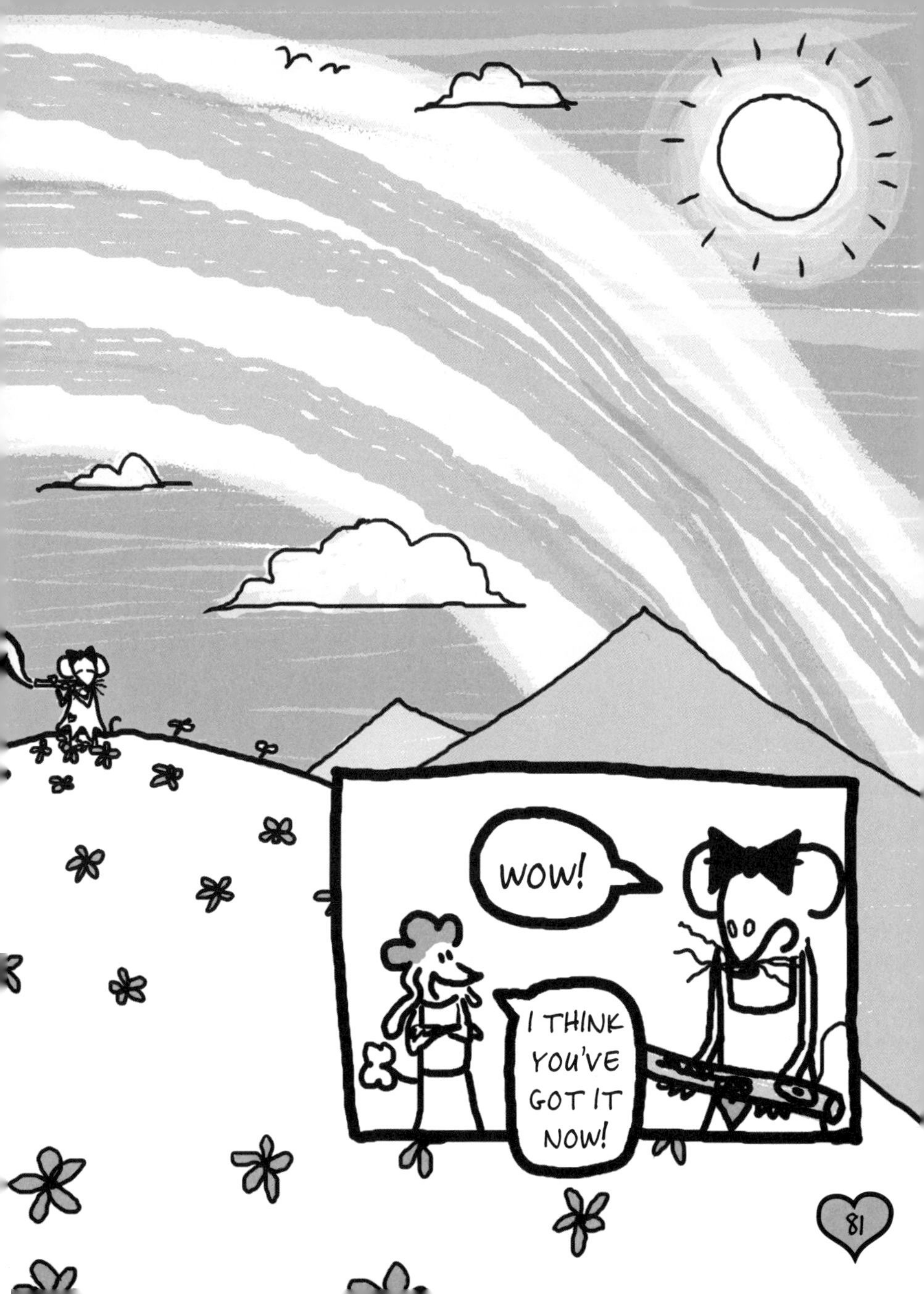
WOW!
I THINK YOU'VE GOT IT NOW!

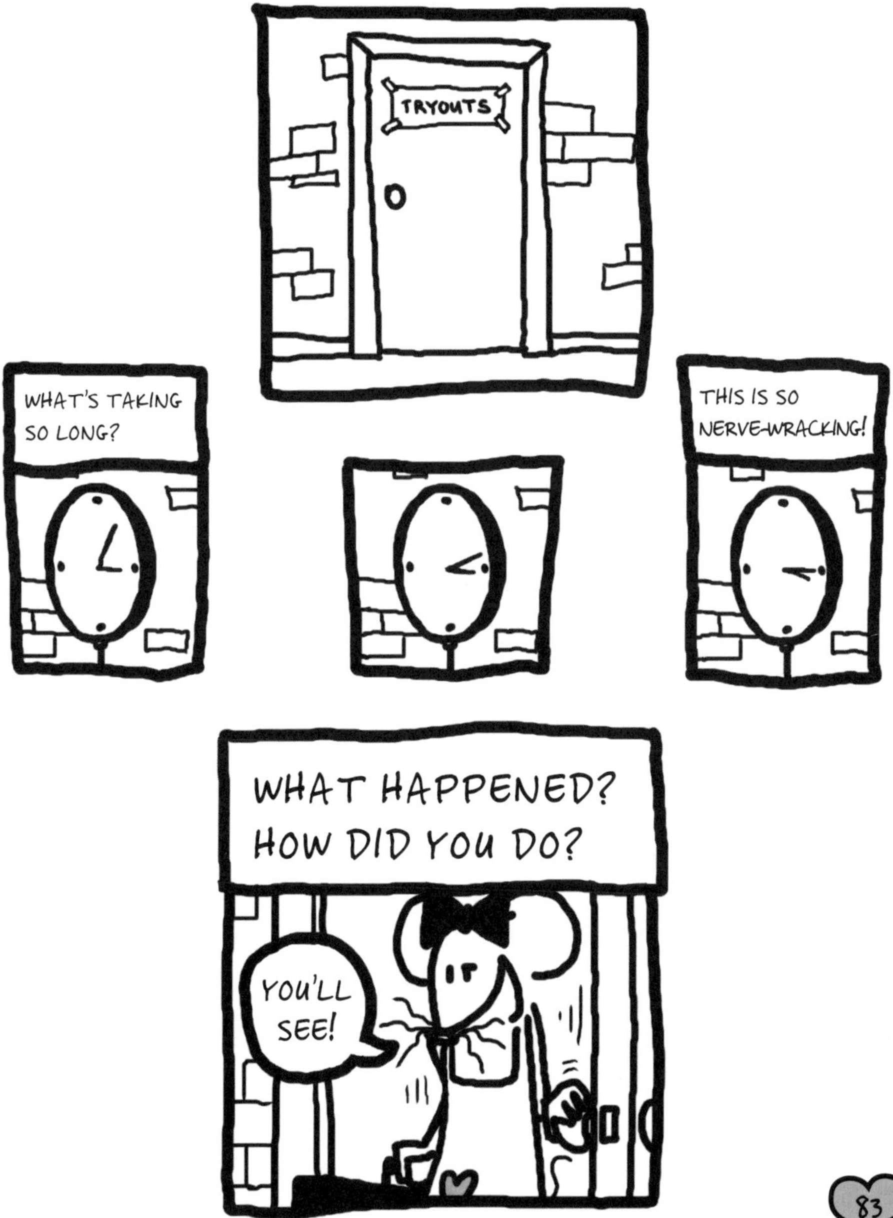
TRYOUTS
WHAT'S TAKING SO LONG?
THIS IS SO NERVE-WRACKING!
WHAT HAPPENED? HOW DID YOU DO?
YOU'LL SEE!

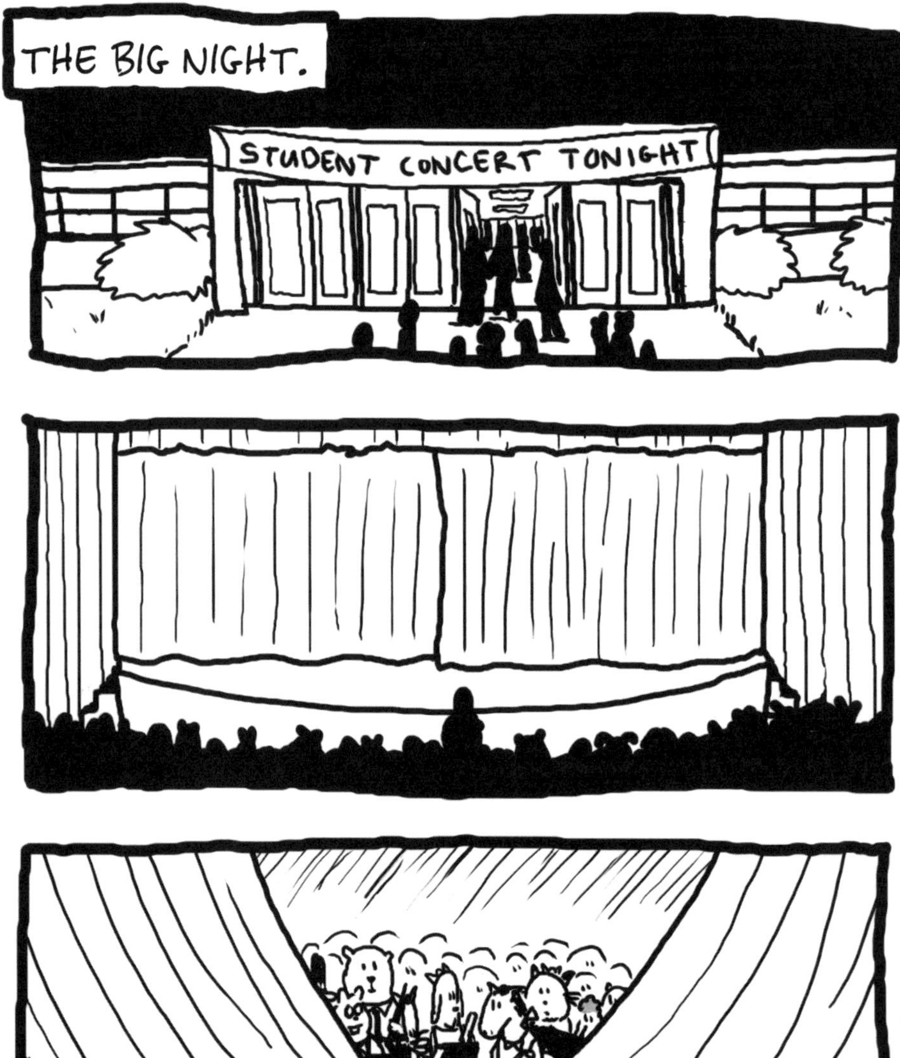
THE BIG NIGHT.
STUDENT CONCERT TONIGHT
SWOOSH!

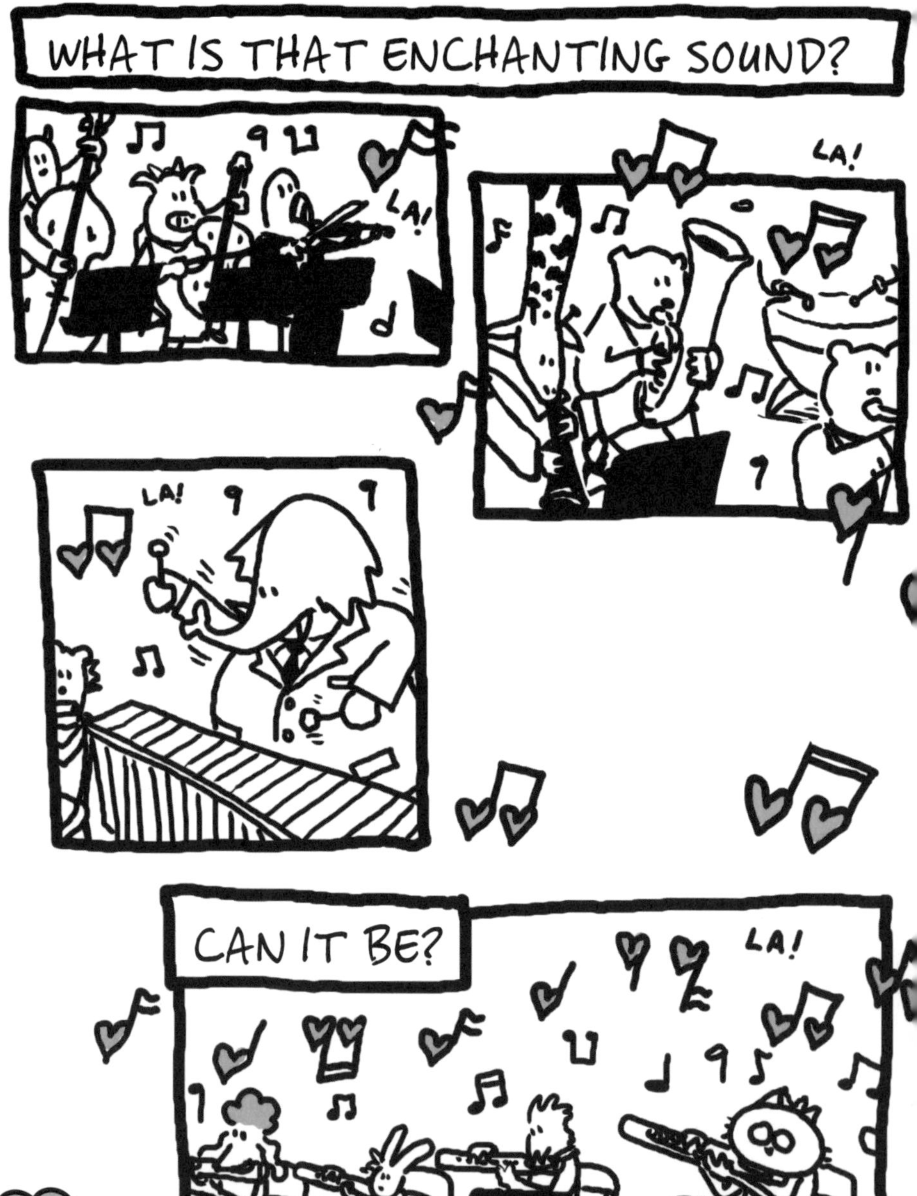
WHAT IS THAT ENCHANTING SOUND?
LA!
LA!
LA!
CAN IT BE?
LA!

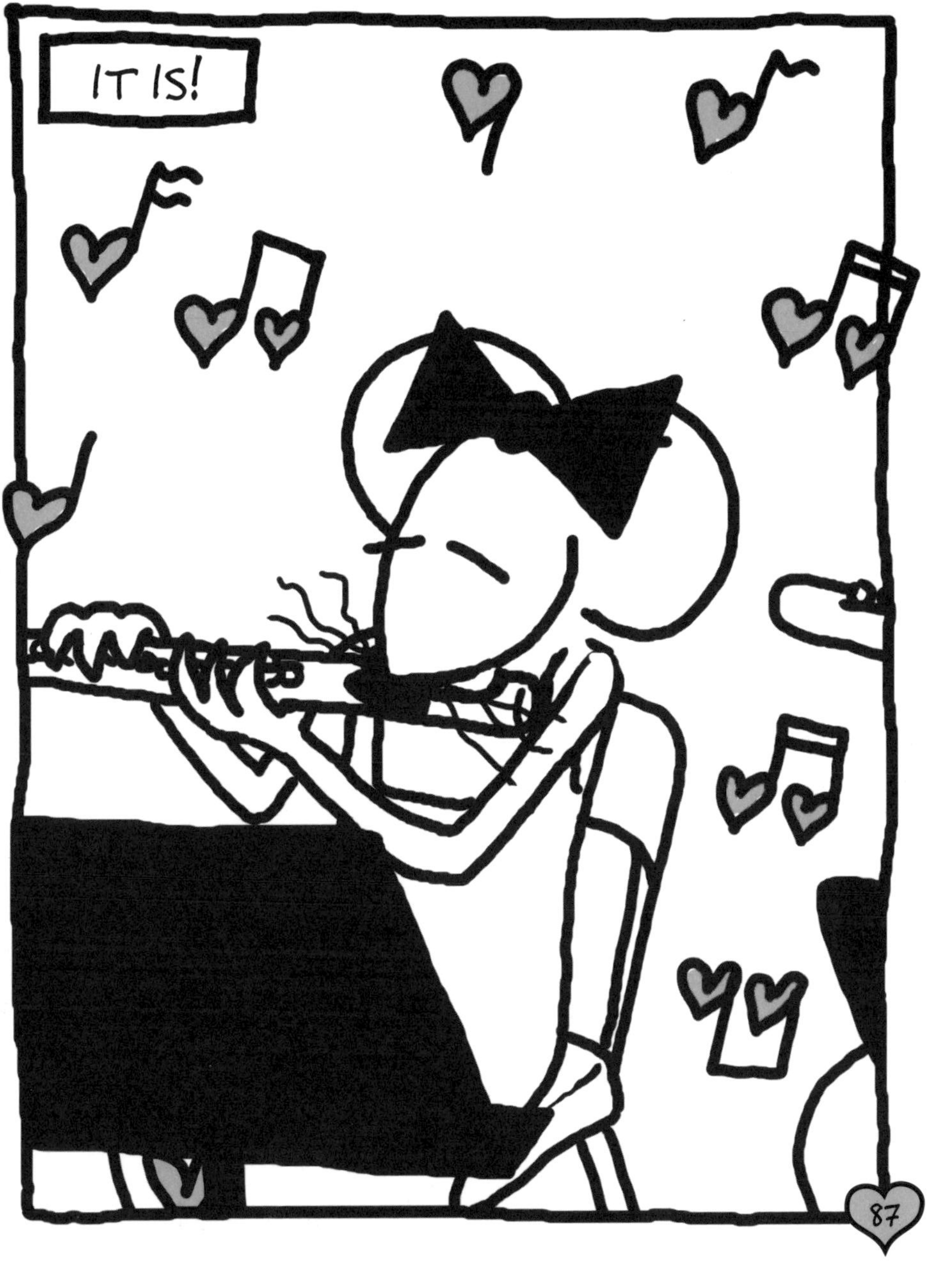
IT IS!

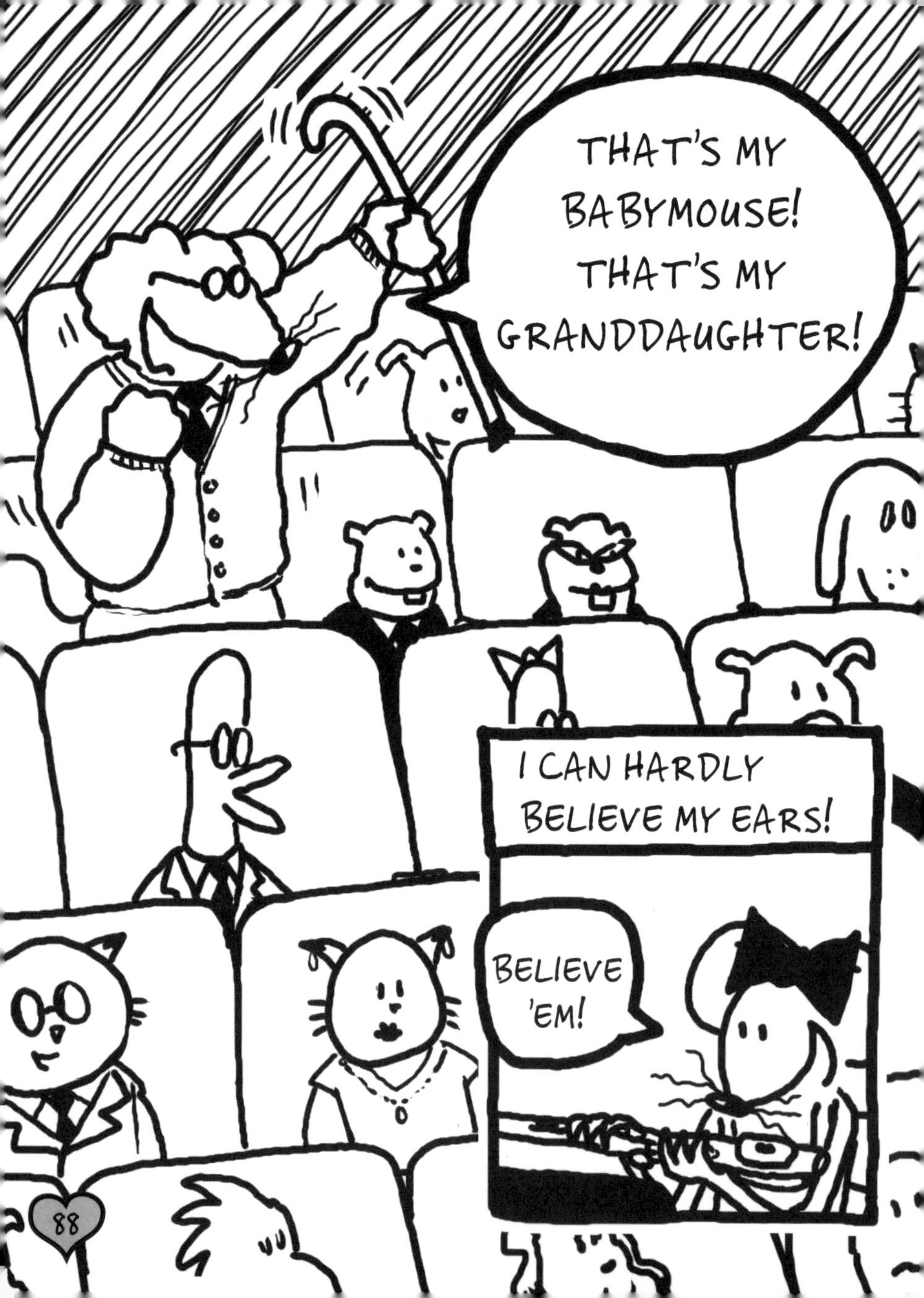
THAT'S MY BABYMOUSE! THAT'S MY GRANDDAUGHTER!
I CAN HARDLY BELIEVE MY EARS!
BELIEVE 'EM!

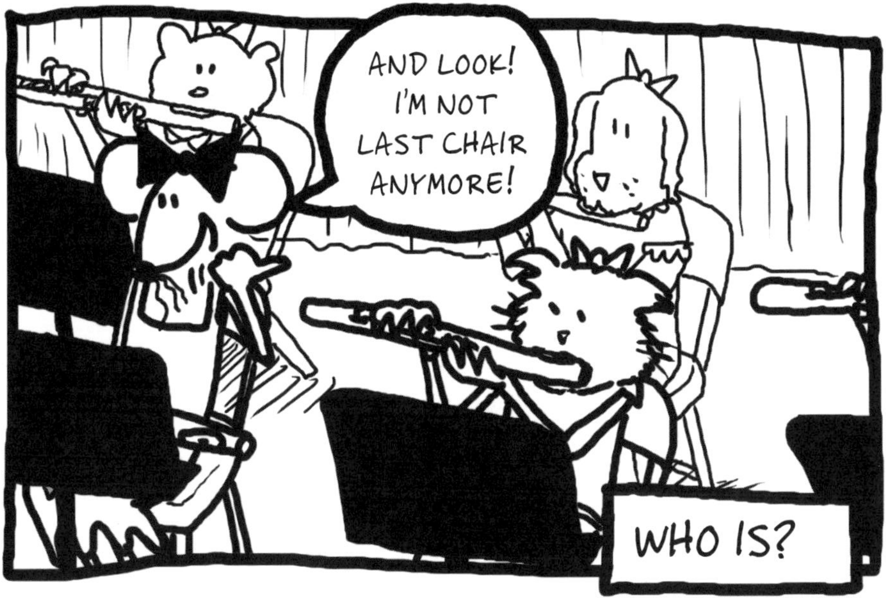
AND LOOK! I'M NOT LAST CHAIR ANYMORE!
WHO IS?

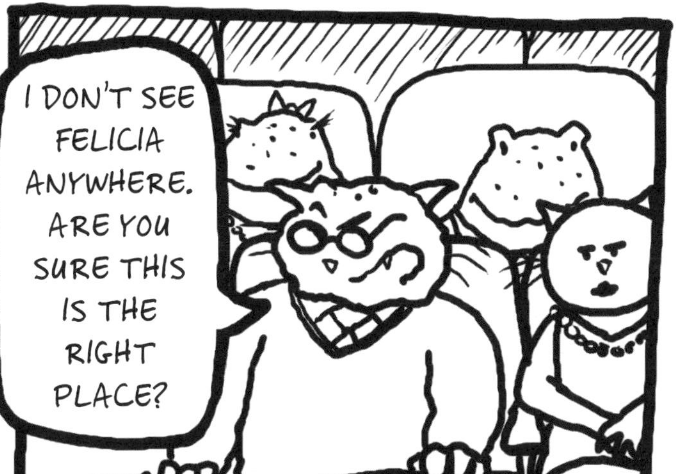
I DON'T SEE FELICIA ANYWHERE. ARE YOU SURE THIS IS THE RIGHT PLACE?

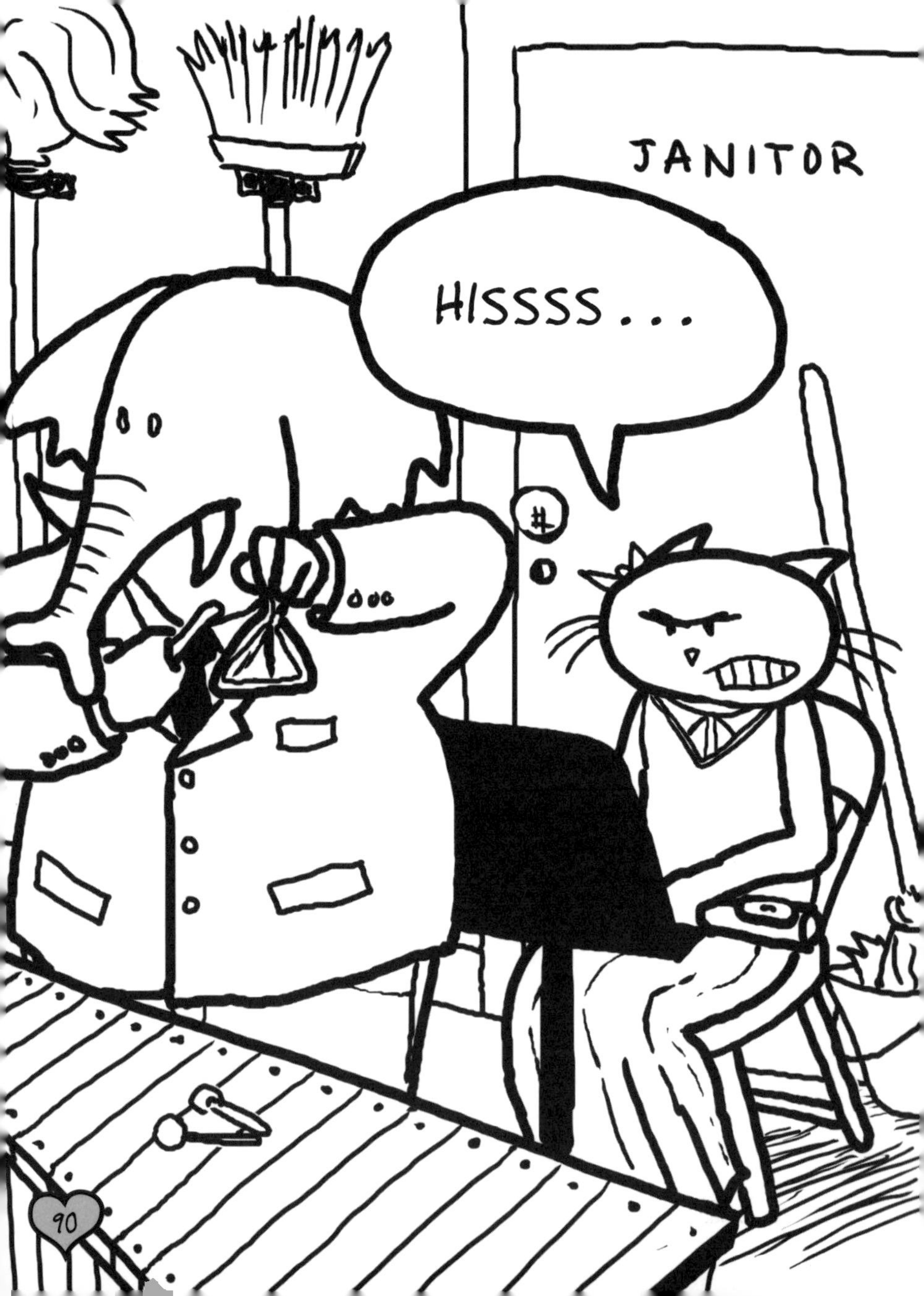
JANITOR
HISSSS . . .

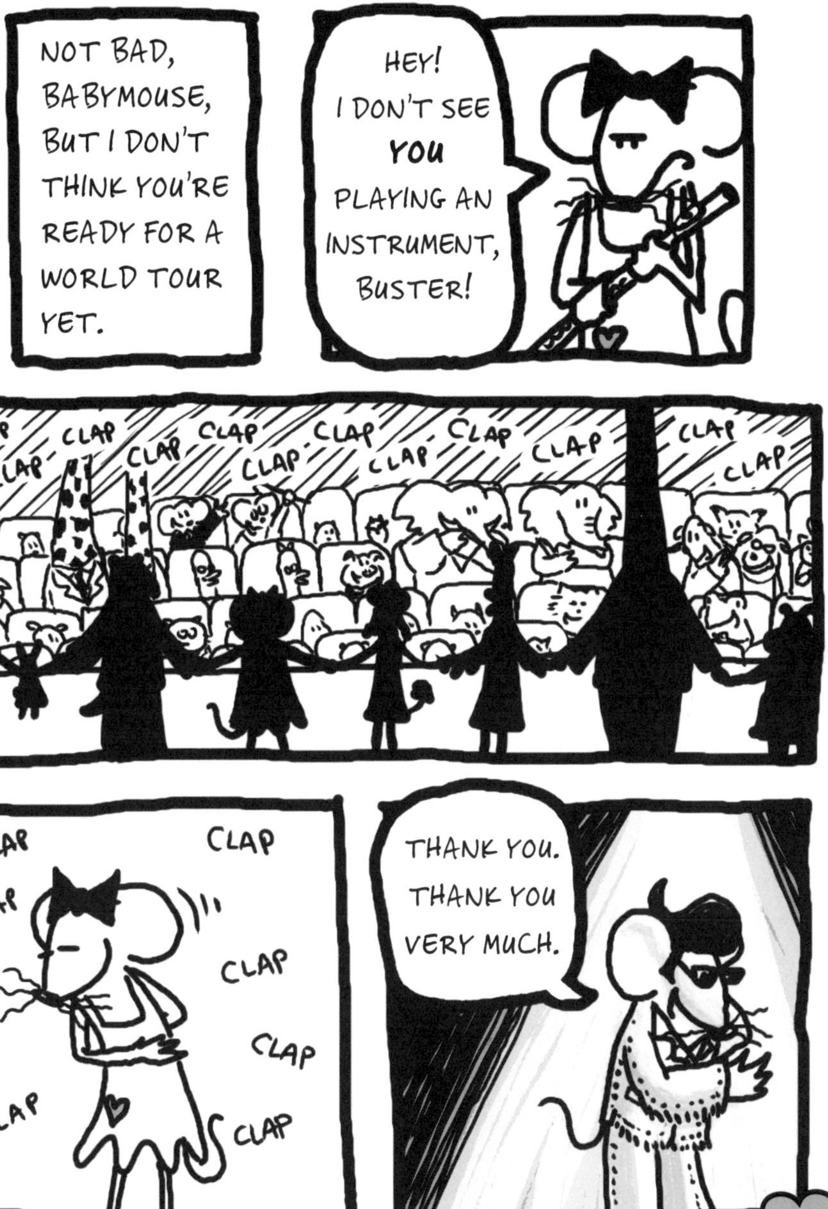
NOT BAD, BABYMOUSE, BUT I DON'T THINK YOU'RE READY FOR A WORLD TOUR YET.
HEY! I DON'T SEE **YOU** PLAYING AN INSTRUMENT, BUSTER!
CLAP
CLAP-CLAP
CLAP
CLAP
CLAP-CLAP
CLAP-CLAP
CLAP
CLAP
CLAP
CLAP
CLAP
CLAP
CLAP
CLAP
CLAP
CLAP
CLAP
THANK YOU. THANK YOU VERY MUCH.

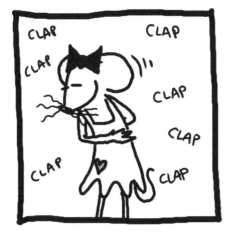

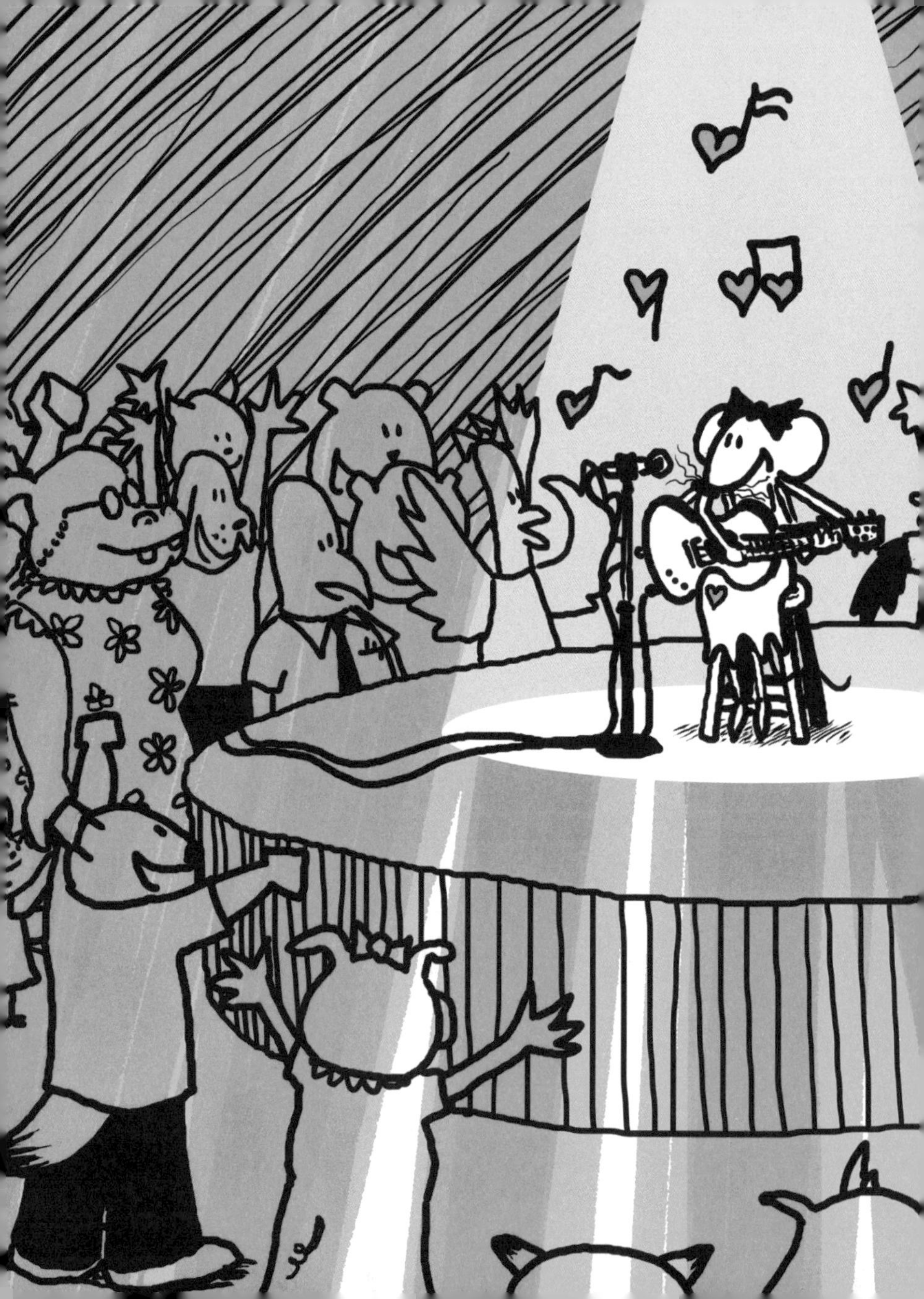

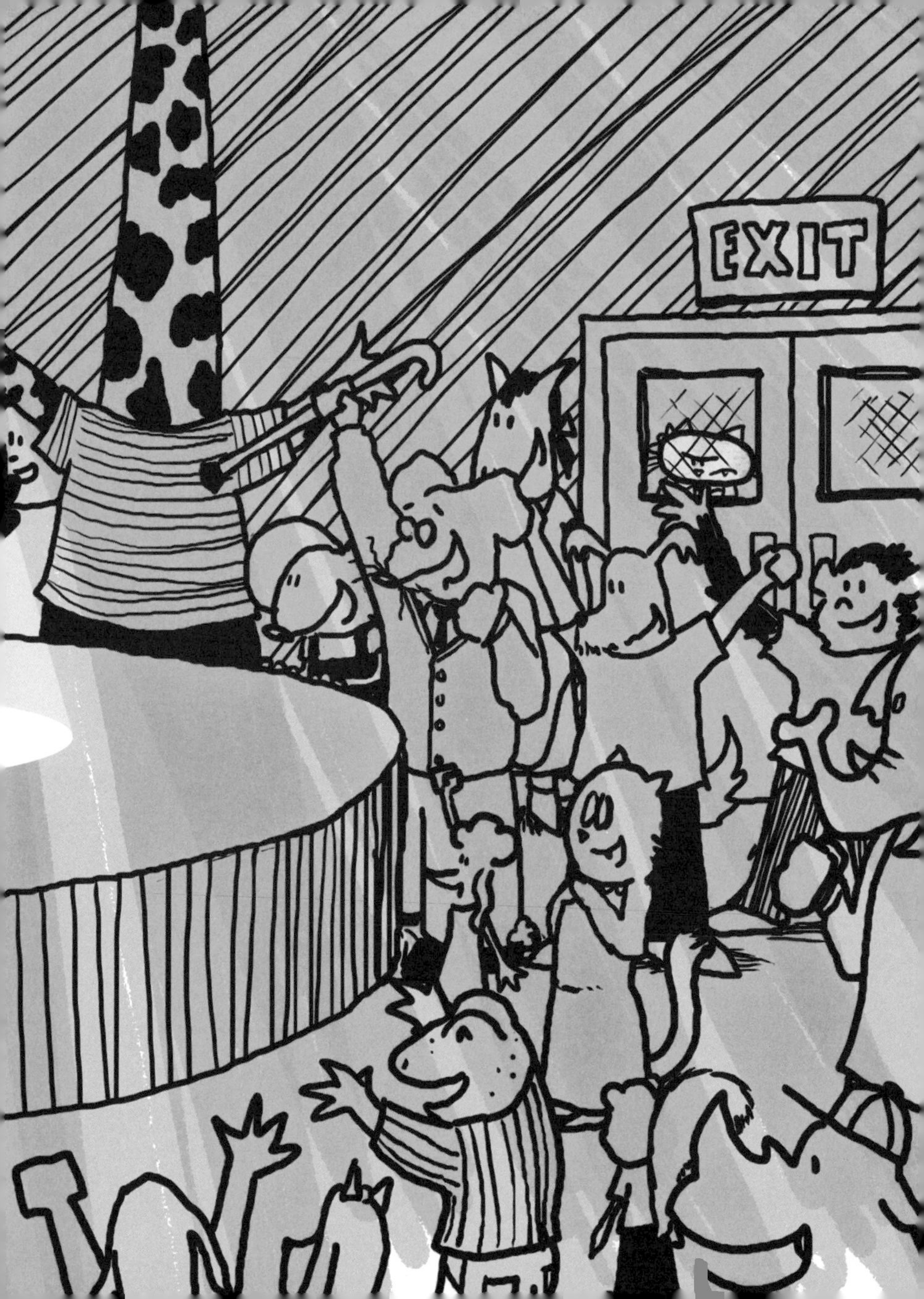
EXIT

GET READY TO FALL IN LOVE...

WITH... BABYMOUSE HEARTBREAKER CRACK!

IN STORES NOW! ♥

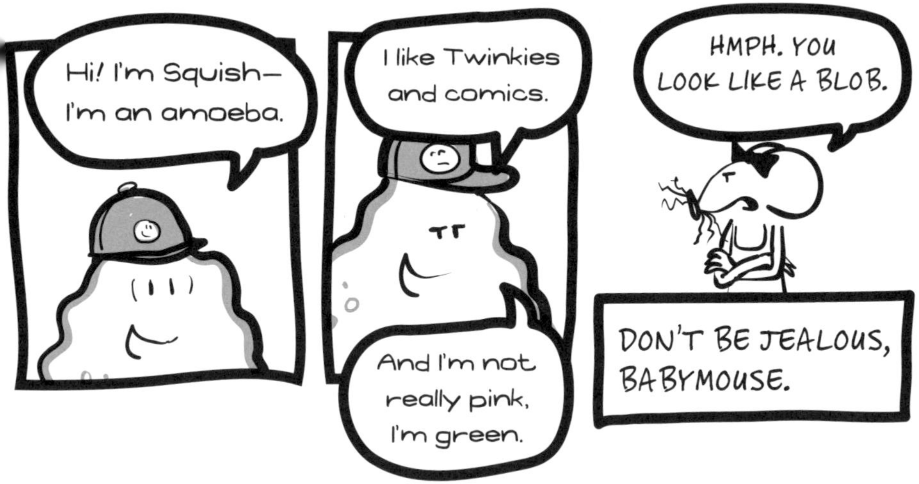
Hi! I'm Squish—
I'm an amoeba.
I like Twinkies and comics.
And I'm not really pink, I'm green.
HMPH. YOU LOOK LIKE A BLOB.
DON'T BE JEALOUS, BABYMOUSE.

READ ABOUT SQUISH'S AMAZING ADVENTURES IN:

#1 SQUISH: Super Amoeba

#2 SQUISH: Brave New Pond

#3 SQUISH: The Power of the Parasite

#4 SQUISH: Captain Disaster

#5 SQUISH: Game On!

#6 SQUISH: Fear the Amoeba

AND COMING SOON:

#7 SQUISH: Deadly DIsease of Doom

★ "IF EVER A NEW SERIES DESERVED TO GO VIRAL, THIS ONE DOES."
—*KIRKUS REVIEWS*, STARRED